# *Pushing the River*

*definition:* a futile attempt
to change the course of events

# Pushing the River

a novel by

Barbara Monier

***Barbara Monier*** loves to hear from readers.

Sign up for her mailing list to receive news
about her latest projects: barbaramonierauthor.com.

You can email her directly at bmonierauthor@yahoo.com.



First Edition ISBN 13: 978-1-937484-65-1

AMIKA PRESS
466 Central AVE #23 Northfield IL 60093 847 920 8084
info@amikapress.com Available for purchase on amikapress.com

Edited by John Manos and Ann Wambach. Cover art by Sarra Jahedi. Cover background photography by David Ritter. Designed and typeset by Sarah Koz. Set in Minion Pro, designed by Robert Slimbach in 1990. Thanks to Nathan Matteson.

Real courage is when you know you're licked
before you begin, but you begin anyway
and see it through no matter what.
—Harper Lee, *To Kill a Mockingbird*

What's the bravest thing you ever did?
He spat in the road a bloody phlegm.
Getting up this morning, he said.
—Cormac McCarthy, *The Road*

# Chapter 1

*I* **have** *lived in the company of ghosts. I have known this for a long time—that I rattled around among specters and spirits and wraiths. But I also knew that they were, indeed, my company.*

*My house, where the vapors lurked, had nine main rooms, not counting baths and laundry and storage and closets. Of those nine rooms, I inhabited five. I used only one of the three baths, one of the six closets, none of the storage areas.*

*A small room off the main part of the basement had been constructed for cold storage when the house was built in 1914. The wooden door at its entrance was at least four inches thick, the door of a vault. An ancient icebox sat inside, which was odd, since an icebox would normally have been kept in the kitchen, or maybe on the back porch. But it came with the house, and we left it where we found it—its bottom compartment open and yawning, forever awaiting the iceman to make his daily rounds, lugging the enormous block of ice that would keep the food cold and fresh for the next twenty-four hours.*

*Every time I entered the room and turned on the light—with its strange, metallic clink—I regretted that we never got around to putting in a regular ceiling light. A bare bulb, hanging from a lopsided wire, lit the pale green walls. I wondered if the floor had once been dirt, if the previous do-it-yourself owner had poured the concrete floor himself.*

*Shelves ran along two sides of the storage room. In one corner of the shelves, the Lionel trains from my childhood lay in their original boxes. People have told me that the old boxes are often as valuable, or even more valuable, than the Lionel trains themselves. But to me, their value came from the fact that playing with the trains, as they wound around the Christmas tree each year of my childhood, was the only moment in my memory that my father ever got down on the floor, on his hands and knees, and smiled the whole time.*

*Different boxes contained a jumble of seemingly unrelated parts and pieces: plastic animals, fake trees, wood lattices, street signs. But I recognized them as remnants of an entire miniature world that my parents created for the trains to pass through: a city zoo; a farm with a house, barn, stables, and animals; a village with buildings that lit from within; and people who sat on park benches under the shade of fluffy trees.*

*In the opposite corner of that shelf, the* HO *trains from my ex-husband Jeff's childhood lay in other boxes—boxes that had been neatly labeled and packed and shipped to us by Jeff's mother. Of his three siblings, Jeff had somehow been designated the Keeper of the Trains. Who knows if it was because of some secret soft spot Jeff's mother had for her only son or for some other reason. Jeff's mother was never one to let many of her thoughts rise to the surface.*

*This was perhaps the only room in the house we never painted. The walls retained the same nondescript green they had on the day we moved in. About two feet off the ground, a faint rust-colored water line wove its way across one wall. I always wondered how it got there—how could water enter this room and make its mark so far above the ground?*

*About half of the basement's height sat underground, and, on occasion, water would gradually insinuate its way from outside to inside—first through the exterior stucco, then through the plaster and wood frame and lath, and finally through the bricks that comprised the basement's interior walls. We fought an eternal battle against crumbling bricks. The walls of our basement regularly blossomed into white, powdery crystals. When the blooms got large and heavy enough, clumps would break off and rain down in piles of chunky dust on the floor.*

*It was remarkable that this one wall—with its painterly line commemorating some event in the history of the house—never changed. I checked it from time to time, to make sure, to marvel at the stubborn permanence the wall bore. It was the same wall that held the shelves that held the trains.*

*Jeff and I were just a couple of wide-eyed kids with a little baby when we moved into this house. John fussed and cried when he wasn't held, so we took turns carrying him. While we scrubbed the floors and painted the walls and dug dirt in the gardens, we tickled and rocked and sang to our baby. He gazed at the world around him like he could stare a hole right through everything and see into its very center. In three years, Kate came along, blonde and golden and fitting right into the universe like it was easy as pie, and every single thing was pure delight.*

*The house felt full. Not just with the family and friends and pets that were constantly coming and going and not just with all the things we gathered and put in different rooms that marked our lives, it was full in the only way that can make a house into a home.*

*Everything seemed to get bigger and bigger. Not just the children, but life itself.*

*When my parents bought their house, the azalea bush directly in front of it was in full, blazing bloom, and my mother was pregnant with me. I know this from a photograph of my parents standing in front of the azalea that spring when I was just a bump on my mother's belly. There is another photo of my mother the very next year when the bush blossomed again, and she is holding a baby just a few months old—the wild-haired infant was me.*

*When John was growing and kicking inside of me, Jeff and I trudged around to place after place—just as my parents had done with the unborn me. I worked so hard to look past the scraps of other people's lives and to gaze ahead, trying to picture if the mortar and brick that stood around us could ever be a true home. Jeff could see the cracks in my hope forming. He would reach for my hand. He would kiss it. "We'll find it, baby. We will."*

*I grew up thinking that this was the way life was meant to be. You grew to adulthood and you found a worthy partner and you started a family and you made a home to raise them in. And you stayed. You weathered whatever came along, and you stayed. You kept right on staying until the moment of your very last breath on Earth, and you did it in the place where you'd lived.*

*Both my mother and my father died at home. My mother, with no warning whatsoever, simply did not wake up one morning. I had talked to her on the phone—twice—the night she died. She went to bed that night the same as every other night, in her big bed in the house where she had spent the first twenty years of my life. She tended the flowers in the beds and washed the drapes once a year like clockwork and made sure her children were dressed and fed and minded their manners. She joined the* PTA *and the church guild and the neighborhood ladies' group that met once a month for a light luncheon and cards.*

*My father had gone upstairs to dress after he'd finished his full pot of coffee and his morning newspaper, and he thought: "That's funny. It sounds like the goddamn alarm clock is buzzing."*

*My mother lay in bed still and peaceful as could be with the alarm clock screaming. My father went over and shook her big toe through the blanket. He called her name into the daytime blackness of the room, the bright July sunlight held back by dense blackout curtains, save for the littlest peek here and there. He went over and pushed the peg of the alarm clock and stood there with his index finger still pressing it, as if he had an inkling that when he took his finger off he would have to figure out what to do next. And, he had the further inkling that this would be the first in a chain of events that marked the beginning of an entirely different life.*

*He shook her toe a few more times and then went over and*

*sat down on his own side of the bed. It occurred to him that maybe if he got back under the covers and shut his eyes for a time and then opened them up again, it might all be different.*

*Eventually he picked up the phone. "Bob," he said, "Bob, I think Mary's dead. I'm not sure, but I think that maybe she is," which was an especially sad and strange thing to say considering my father was a doctor and he knew through and through that my mother would never take another breath.*

*Five years after that, my father was a shadow of his former self. He spent most of that five years sitting in one chair, at the table in the dining room. From that chair, he sorted through his piles of mail and leafed through his magazines and sipped at his bowls of lukewarm broth and watched whatever happened to be on the television. He drank—a lot—and he smoked so much that the walls of the house, which had been painted a bright, eggshell white under my mother's watch, became coated in a sickly bronze. He ate nothing but canned soup: chicken noodle or cream of mushroom. He drank his whiskey straight in big tumblers with his initials etched in a diamond pattern, glasses my parents had gotten as a wedding present. The callus on his thumb was substantial from running it across the letter* M, *over and over, the one initial they had in common.*

*His hands shook, his lungs and his liver were shot, and he could barely sense the ground underneath him because he could no longer feel his feet. But worst of all for him, his eyesight was nearly gone, so he could no longer see to read his beloved newspaper. He drank his pot of coffee and smoked a great many cigarettes each morning while squinting at his paper, holding it close to one eye first and then the other; but the news on* TV *was giving him all the information he got, really. The man who had gotten down on his hands and knees to play with the Lionel trains, who had painstakingly built a mountain—complete with a tunnel for the trains to pass through—and a lake, well, that man had vanished, piece by slow piece.*

*When my twenty-five-year marriage to Jeff ended, I asked him if he wanted the trains. I asked him several times. He always said yes; but he never came to claim them. Eventually he moved far away, and the trains remained in their neatly packed boxes, shipped at great expense from his parents' house in West Virginia.*

*So many things have been just like this for me—the shards and shreds of a life gone by. Like all people who marry, we came from two separate families, and we joined together to make our own new family. I became the Keeper of the Trains, a role I chose freely, without burden or regret—because I understood that there might come a time when someone would want those trains.*

*I lived among closets filled with the history of others, because any of the things within them might be needed at any time. Or perhaps the rooms themselves might be needed, as they had been many, many times as my children—and several of their roommates and friends and significant others and spouses—needed a place to live, to call home.*

*It is possible that they will not need this again from me. It is more likely, in fact, that the time will come, as I move toward my twilight, that I might need sanctuary from them.*

*In the meantime, I rattled around a great deal of space, just in case that space might be needed.*

*It's the first day of September 2012, and I have been living alone for a long time. When Jeff first left—fourteen years ago today—I could read without glasses even the smallest print on the train boxes. When my hands reached up to dust those boxes, the craggy blue veins did not stand out starkly against my sallow hands. The skin did not pucker into fascinating, horrifying patterns that measure my years.*

*When John left for college eleven years ago, I had three more years in the house with Kate. Since she left, it has been just me.*

*Yes, I have lived in the company of ghosts. I knew well what they were. But I also knew that they were, indeed, company.*

## Chapter 2

*Madeline* had only one contact when she and Jeff moved to Chicago at ripe summer's end of 1980; but that one contact led to a job and that job led her to Ellie. They were both twenty-four years old. Ellie's unfettered laugh and her crazy waist-length braids and her spectrum of facial expressions immediately drew Madeline into a friendship. They reclaimed their childhood love of ballet together and met for two or three dance classes a week. They learned how to knit together, compared patterns and stitches, and helped repair one another's mistakes. Bad days at work, or good ones, were often followed by a glass of wine at their favorite neighborhood pub. Ellie was a self-proclaimed lightweight as a drinker, and Madeline was completely charmed by how quickly Ellie's spirits could rise to buoyant and beyond. Ellie threw her head back with hearty laughter and tossed around her crayon-yellow blonde hair.

They weathered the next thirty-one years together, through everything that happened in their lives: the births of five children, the deaths of three parents and two brothers, and the breaking apart of one of their families. All of it.

It was with Ellie that Madeline took a walk on the morning of September 1st. Ellie asked if Madeline would meet at the sculpture park, a path of several miles that wound along a creek and through both open, grassy spaces and shady, wooded thickets. Though the park was within Madeline's town, she had walked it only once before. Madeline had genuinely liked the experience of wandering the path and examining the large, highly varied sculptures, but she had just never returned. *I am so much a creature of habit,* Madeline thought. *The lake is close; I go to the lake.*

Long before Jeff moved to his new apartment on the first day of September, Madeline had associated the date with a new year—much more so than January 1. The shift of the seasons, the smell of fresh school supplies, the whirl of upcoming holidays, filled Madeline with a sense of anticipation and possibility.

Madeline greeted Ellie with this heady outlook. Hope floated inside Madeline like an infusion of oxygen as they embarked on the path and dove into a breathless catch-up. The feeling burst immediately when the subject turned to dating.

"Ellie, what in the world am I going to do?" Madeline said.

"You," Ellie said, "are going to take a much-needed break from what you've been trying to do ever since Jeff left—the single-minded 'project' you have made out of dating. The mission to secure a new 'forever.' "

"Huh," Madeline said, in the particular deadpan way that

had been their thirty-year private joke. Madeline had adopted Ellie's go-to response, the one Ellie used to indicate that what the other person had just said was baffling, confounding, or hopelessly irrational.

"It's time," Ellie said. "You need the break."

"Huh."

"I think this will be a great thing."

"Huh." Madeline added, "I think *you* need the break."

"OK, perhaps we both do."

How many walks just like this one had Ellie and Madeline taken over the past ten years since Jeff left? Madeline wondered. How many times had they clipped along on some pathway, beachfront, nature preserve, or botanic garden? How many cups of coffee had been sipped in little cafés, student centers, large malls, or bookstores, while they deconstructed Madeline's latest date, possible romance, new romance, budding relationship, full! rosy! cheeked! blush! of! love! first stagger, swaying, reeling, crumbling, dissolving, dissolving, dissolved.

The thought of all this exhausted Madeline. She was utterly bored with herself. Bored and worn-out and miserable about how much time and brain space and thought and conversation the whole subject of dating and relationships had sucked from her life. She had a nearly overwhelming desire to lie down in the grass right then, halfway along the trail, right there, in the middle of the sculpture garden, and resolve to stay there, not move, not continue, until something changed. The blades of grass would soak up the late summer sun and caress her with their easy warmth. She would watch the wispy clouds drift lazily across the sky; she would search for the pictures in them, then make up elaborate stories out of the pictures. The air would turn cool, and the leaves would start to change, just barely at first, a tinge of color lost. The gathering autumn winds would tease the leaves from the trees and toss them in swirls and cyclones of gold. Cyclists would whiz past her as she lay perfectly still, thinking, "I believe they have added a new sculpture to the garden." The first tiny, barely perceptible flake of snow would drift onto her cheek—

"You're not rethinking this, are you?" Ellie said.

For less than half a second Madeline considered telling Ellie what she had been thinking, but she said, "No. I'm not."

"Good. Be here now," Ellie said.

"OK, then. With you as my witness, I resolve to go back online, to once again enter the fray of online dating. But for the first time since Jeff left, I resolve not to think about 'forever,' but to...what you said...be here now."

## Chapter 3

It was not her first foray into the parallel universe of online dating. Madeline had been divorced for more than ten years. She had braved a string of relationships that progressed from interest to the first tingle of excitement, to the exhilaration of genuine possibility, to the frightening, heady, joyful moment when the roller coaster passed the peak of its climb and, in that split second, there was no going back: momentum had taken over. It was utterly and completely out of anyone's control, because at that moment, there was love. There was real love.

And then, there wasn't.

Madeline took time to lick the wounds of disappointment. She allowed the lesions of dashed hopes to scab over. She understood that persevering was an ongoing matter of sustaining one's optimism just enough ahead of the injury of experience to keep going.

After a time she would go back online, pouring over profiles, scrutinizing descriptions, gathering courage. As crazy a universe as online dating was—she recalled a friend aptly calling it the Wild West, meaning a vast land where there are no rules, lots of very bad behavior, some good souls, and the possibility that absolutely anything can happen—it was essentially the only path to meet people. Since Madeline worked alone, never buddied up to men in bars, and didn't attend church, she reconciled herself to the necessary methodology.

Madeline had believed herself to be a seasoned and skilled decipherer of online profiles; consequently, in prior online forays, she had been highly selective in communicating with anyone. She considered this not snobbery, but a serious matter of saving both parties additional wear and tear on their fragile senses of hope.

She decided that this time around she would do things differently. She would write an e-mail response to each and every person who had taken the time to write to her, just as the daughter of Mary Barbara Mills had been taught to do as a necessary part of maintaining a civilized society.

Madeline ventured onto a dating site she had never tried before.

Within a few short days, the un-wisdom of her approach had become painfully clear.

The very first e-mail she received was from a man who seemed quite decent and worked in an educational consulting field similar to her own. Madeline thanked him for writing but said that she endeavored to find someone in an entirely different line of work, to assure some balance, and she wished him well. In response, he argued with her, bullied her, called her names, and hurled a few insults. Prepared as she had believed she was for the maelstrom of online dating, Madeline was stunned by the intensity of rage this guy had unleashed on a total stranger.

Later that same day, she received a first message from a man who seemed...pretty good. Cute, a bit off the beaten path, fun loving and witty, and seeming to be genuinely seeking something of substance in both a woman and a relationship. Madeline responded, and the two of them "chatted" back and forth —anonymously through the site—throughout the afternoon. At one point he asked Madeline what she did for work; she responded that she did educational consulting for at-risk families. He wrote back: "It's completely unhealthy to spend time with people less fortunate than ourselves."

Earlier in her life, Madeline would have assumed that he was joking. She may have laughed. But, lo these many years of life later, she instead wrote back and asked: "Are you serious?" He replied: "Absolutely, yes. That has been my experience."

Madeline thought: *Ok. Deep breath. Wild West. Onward.*

A new message appeared from him: "I mean, these people have undoubtedly stolen from you, right?"

Madeline took the rest of the night off.

The next morning, she received an e-mail from a guy with a wonderful, open smile. He had lots of photos of himself at various charity events looking very dapper and sincere, a give-back sort of a guy. A few e-mail exchanges led to their mutual decision to text message via the site.

"Both parents born in Italy. You?" he asked Madeline.

"My father was 100 percent French, first generation. My mother was essentially a WASP."

"Are you Jewish?"

*Wait, are there people who honestly don't know what WASP means? Is he double-checking if I perhaps converted at some point?*

Madeline wrote, "No."

"Good."

"Why?"

"I don't get along with Jewish women."

*Here I am again, asking for the second time in as many days:* "Are you serious?"

"Yes. They're whiny, nasally, pretentious, drama-filled, high maintenance, boring."

Madeline stopped writing, but a few minutes later a final text appeared.

"Also, they never ever take their wallets out to buy a man a drink. In other words they're cheap as shit."

*Ten deep breaths. Crazy Wild West. Onward.*

## *Chapter 4*

*My mother thought of herself as a beautiful woman. I'm not sure how I knew this, but I was certain of it: she went through each day of her life with the confident certainty that her beauty was a given. She never spoke of this and referred to it only once that I can remember. When I was a teenager, maybe fourteen or fifteen, and boys had begun to sniff and circle around our house, my mother said one day, out of the blue: "You definitely have the better body, but I believe that I have the prettier face."*

*Even then, in my dewy youth, I thought: "What a weird-ass thing to say."*

*Many years ago I worked with a Chicago theater ensemble. As ensembles are wont to do, we made every effort to cast our play productions from within our own pool of ten or so actors. An enormous pool of talent existed there, but some of the corps were definitely more versatile in their range than others. None was more versatile than Lindsay. She was a chameleon.*

*When she walked in off the street, with her colorless platinum* hair, pale blue eyes, and inevitable cigarette, Lindsay projected the demeanor of someone whose strong preference was to remain unnoticed. With an outward air that contradicted her stage aspirations, Lindsay was a bundle of contrasts. She offered her greeting—her Lindsay smile, with the slight overbite that made her teeth linger on her upper lip—then took her seat and immediately seemed to recede, as if she were striving to become one with the chair that held her. Lindsay could use this trait to amazing advantage on the stage, in roles where she could appear—no, be—so worn and weary and shriveled up into some deep phantom of a former self, it seemed utterly impossible that she could actually be a woman in her mid-twenties. Or, Lindsay could walk onto the stage and take your breath away. She was radiant, stunning, utterly beautiful.

Lindsay created strong echoes of my mother, for this was the very quality my mother possessed—whatever this is. There exists this thing that comes from some well deep within, this quality of being that is able to convince anyone who looks upon you that you are, in every way, beautiful.

My mother never worked at being beautiful and, in fact, would have considered the effort a ridiculous waste of time and a bewildering, superficial focus. She came of age in the late 1930s and early '40s, when the makeup regimen of a serious, athletic college girl consisted of dabbing a puff of compact powder on both sides of her nose—exactly twice—and applying a good coat of lipstick.

My mother took very little time to get ready each morning. A couple of fast brush strokes through her hair, dab dab on her *nose, a quick and artfully drawn mouth, and a glance at both sides of her face. But like Lindsay preparing for the stage, by the time she finished this simple routine, a beautiful woman stared back at her in the mirror.*

*Over the two decades that my mother and I cohabited the planet, her beauty regimen changed very little. The only dramatic change occurred when she switched from doing her hair herself—in the style she had worn since college—to having it "done" each week at a salon. She chose a style that was highly constructed and bore no relationship to anything hair would ever do on its own, but it would last a full week between salon visits and look astonishingly unchanged. Sometimes I would lie in bed and think about her hair remaining unwashed for an entire week. And looking the same! Occasionally I dreamed of plants starting to grow in my own hair that I would have to painstakingly pull out of my scalp, making sure to get the entire root without breaking the little sprigs. Also, I never really knew what my father thought of the change. He was fond of saying, "Women never look better than the moment they step out of the shower." Now that I think about it, that was probably an exceptional gift for my father to have given me. He added, "All this stuff that women do—with their hair and their makeup and their dress—it's all done for each other, for what other women think. Men don't like any of it."*

*But by then my mother had discovered the great joy that many women of the time experienced—the weekly visit to the hairdresser! She returned with her hair curled and teased and lacquered in place, displaying bubbly good spirits that carried through the rest of the day. Each week she would regale us with new tales of Don and Gretta, the husband and wife owners of the shop. Don was apparently chatty, convivial, and completely nonthreatening to his married female clientele—a charmer anyone would want to tell her troubles and secrets to. By early 1960s, suburban Pittsburgh, Pennsylvania, standards, Gretta was Glamor itself—meaning she came off as adorable (rather than trashy or cheap) in her platinum-hair, cat-eye-makeup, slim-figure, capri-sporting way. She was quiet, letting Don do the heavy lifting of the conversing. Quite slender and petite, she also gave the impression of perhaps just a hint of fragility, a hint that expanded considerably once she experienced a number of Tragic Miscarriages. My mother was all aflutter about poor Gretta, taking each of the miscarriages, and Greta's increasing quiet, totally to heart. When my mother received news of a third miscarriage, I came home from school to an open bottle of Anacin on the kitchen counter alongside a note saying she had taken to her bed, but that she had every intention of rallying in time to have supper on the table at the usual stroke of six o'clock.*

*Gretta never did carry a pregnancy to term; she and Don never had a baby. But her tragic situation touched the hearts of her middle-aged patronage deeply. Meaning, business boomed. She and Don expanded into a brand-new shop with considerably more space and more staff, and they began carrying a wide array of beauty products—including makeup.*

*Sadly, perhaps, this coincided with my own entrance into the 1960s. In junior high, as it was called back then, I endured the torture of setting my stick-straight hair in rollers that I slept on* at night, even though my hair would invariably revert to its natural state well before I got anywhere near school. But I liked to think that I looked mighty fine at the bus stop, and perhaps for a portion of homeroom as well. At the ripe old ages of twelve and thirteen, I never left the house without a chic coat of mascara and nearly white lipstick. And, if I were wearing a dress or skirt (which I was every day at school, since girls wearing pants was still a dream for the future), I wore a girdle. A girdle. At thirteen. WE ALL DID. And if you don't think you've come a long way, baby, think about that girdle thing one more time.

Everything changed in my thirteenth year. Before my fourteenth birthday, I had tossed out my last jar of Dippity-do, deep-sixed my hair curlers, and thrown away a large number of white, pink-white, and nearly white tubes of frosted lipstick. Although I was slightly late to the party, it was Pittsburgh, Pennsylvania, in 1969, and I considered myself a Hippie. I pared my wardrobe down to one pair of jeans that were long enough to abrade the bottoms in an artful fashion, a pair of moccasins that I wore in all weather conditions, four identical mock turtleneck sweaters in different colors for winter, and four men's T-shirts for summer.

Suddenly everyone who had been desperately trying to get their hair to hold a curl was straightening it! I grew my hair to my waist and beamed when people asked me, as they did regularly, if I ironed it to get it so straight. I was a Natural Woman. I told my mother she had given me her last Toni home permanent, thank you very much, and gathered up my bras for a ritual burning. My mother was actually quite accepting of the changes in My Look, never getting especially excited when I came home *with frozen feet from wearing moccasins in mid-winter or put the same pair of jeans in the laundry time after time (though jeans were not meant to look clean at this time—we doodled on them with ink pens, and, if we didn't smoke ourselves, we borrowed friends' cigarettes so we could grind the ashes into our jeans and create a look that was just so).*

*My mother drew the line at the bra thing, however. She commenced ongoing, anatomical lectures about the Cooper's ligament and how I was putting myself and my fourteen-year-old breasts in danger of developing a ghastly condition known as Cooper's Droop, due to my poor, braless B-size breasts being un-able to support their own massive weight and the ligaments stretching under the immense strain and ending up with...Cooper's Droop. Her own mother had suffered this fate, she told me. Being a fashion victim of the 1920s, the flapper era when women's ideal appearance was flat chested, my grandmother had actually bound her ample bosom, resulting in...Cooper's Droop. My mother alleged that things degenerated to the point where my grandmother had to lift her breasts out of the way in order to fasten her belt. My mother attempted to horrify me even further by saying that at least it was easier for my grandmother to see the breast lumps she kept developing.*

*I was unfazed. Cooper's Droop be damned. My girls were set free.*

*Meanwhile, my mother came home from her weekly hair appointments sporting a face that seemed only vaguely reminiscent of the one she had left the house with. In her eagerness to embrace the day and to sell her wares, Gretta sent my mother home each week with shockingly inappropriate eye makeup and a passel of samples. We tried to be kind. But the colors that were smeared across my mother's eyelids were truly an assault on both nature and my mother.*

*My mother never did "do" her eyes on a daily basis, but on the rare occasions when she and my father went out for the evening, she would spread Gretta's samples across her bathroom counter, stand in front of her room-sized mirror, and attack the job at hand in much the same way that she attacked gardening. My mother had no eyelashes—well, damn few, in the sense that what hairs did manage to sprout forth happened to be sparse, fine, blond, and exceptionally short. Nevertheless, my mother would grab her eyelash curler (a medieval contraption I tried a handful of times to largely painful and highly undesired results, meaning I either ripped out more eyelashes than I curled, or I ended up with lashes that formed a severe right angle) with no end of determination for the task at hand.*

*Mascara of the day bore little resemblance to the technological marvels of lengthening, thickening, volumizing, curling, smudge-proofing, waterproofing, lash-defining, non-clumping, lash-separating types that incorporate resins, waxes, nylon fibers, and light-reflecting particles that overwhelm us today. My mother's mascara was a brownish goo that I'm pretty sure was actually a combination of shoe polish and cold cream. The applicator wand was essentially a screw, much like one would find at the local hardware store, and the tarry goo insinuated itself between the threads of the screw. Once my mother had curled her lashes, swiped the mascara screw across their length, then repeated the entire process a second time...well, it's difficult to describe the end result. It did look as if my mother had something coming out from the edges of her eyelids—not eyelashes, exactly, but something.*

*My mother relished the idea that Gretta's little eye shadow samples had taken a page directly from Elizabeth Taylor's 1963 role as Cleopatra. Like Gretta's miscarriages, my mother followed the news of Taylor's frightening health scare that nearly ruined the movie's production, her great love affair with Richard Burton, and the charming fact that once married she referred to herself as Betty Burton. So. My mother stood before me, clumps of...something on her lash line where her real lashes had once been, colors that could scarcely be imagined swathed across her lids, and, as a final touch, a kiss of lipstick in one of the exact pale, frosted shades that I had recently tossed away. In her gown, and her glory, my mother asked me how she looked.*

*I loved my mother. I said she looked just swell.*

*And now, as I get ready for a date of my own, the image staring back at me from the mirror is a woman in her mid-fifties. I am the same age that my mother was when she asked me that question.*

## Chapter 5

*Madeline* worked hard to extinguish the flame she had carried for Jeff. But the feeling of being part of something larger than herself—everything from the ongoing sense that life was bigger and mattered more, to the immeasurable joy of small, everyday moments—was a living spirit inside of her that fueled her dispiriting dating efforts.

Finally, someone who wrote caught her eye. She wrote back and felt a flutter in her belly when she saw his username in her e-mail inbox once again. A lively written exchange between her new Gentleman Caller and herself convinced Madeline that he was well worth meeting.

They agreed to meet for a drink. He wanted her to pick the spot and said something about knowing she would choose a great neighborhood place with "real people" that wasn't "too bourgeois." *Fuck,* Madeline thought, *what are real people?! Plus, it's the fucking suburbs—it's bourgeois by definition, for God's sake.*

Madeline researched with a vengeance, studying descriptions and photos from her Google search of "neighborhood bars." When she walked the two miles from her house to the Beacon Tavern, her first thought was: *Wow, I hope they paid that photographer about a million bucks for making this joint look like it was actually cool.* The Beacon was a haphazard mishmash. It looked as if someone had collected a bunch of random stuff with a vaguely nautical theme, dumped it here and there, and was too lazy to do anything further. *How can this bar be so crowded and still generate such a feeling of loneliness?* An ungodly number of forlorn-looking people jammed the bar, making the throbbing lights and house music seem thoroughly pathetic, as well as laughably out of sync with the quasi-nautical decor. Even the bartender looked as if she would rather be somewhere else.

A first glance around the room didn't turn up anyone Madeline thought resembled his online picture. Certainly nobody came close to what her daughter-in-law Claire had called the Underwear Model upon seeing his photo. "Oh! My! God! He's an underwear model!"

"Do you know if there's anybody here waiting for somebody? A guy?" she screamed at the bartender, leaning over the bar as far as she possibly could in order to be heard.

"Ha," the bartender retorted, "I'm pretty sure everybody here is waiting for somebody."

Perhaps it was Madeline's doleful, hopeful expression that caused the bartender to do a one-eighty from jaded cynic to compassionate sob sister. "I mean, not that I know of, honey. You're just gonna have to look."

"Yeah. Thanks."

And then Madeline saw him. Quantum Leap. Standing in a dark shadow next to the door, pressed against the back wall as if pinned there, minutely nodding his head in time to the music in a good-soldier effort to not look as thoroughly uncomfortable as he clearly was. *Wow, he must have snuck in during the ten seconds I was talking to the bartender and not been so sure if he wanted to stay.*

Because Dan had been scanning the other side of the room and had not yet spotted her, Madeline got a long, private first glance at him. Off-white, baggy, mid-calf-length shorts that spanned an arc encompassing both gangsta and J.Crew. Collared shirt. *Collared shirt? I did not see that coming.* She had pictured T-shirt. Very faded. Possibly with the name of an early punk band, but more likely touting some esoteric, highly left-leaning thing. Noam Chomsky, maybe. And, not only was the shirt collared, it was striped. So boldly striped, in fact, that Madeline's mind leapt to the time a new Chicago colleague said to her: "You're not from around here are you?" based on his observation that she exclusively wore the subdued tones of an East Coast native. Dan, she knew from the flurry of e-mails that preceded this plunge into an in-person meeting, had grown up in the city of Chicago.

"Dan?" she yelled.

He was tall. Six foot three, maybe even six foot four; even at five foot nine, Madeline had to balance on the tips of her toes to get his ear in the general vicinity of her mouth. He nodded, minimally, in time to the music, as if he were not sure he wanted to acknowledge his identity to the person who had chosen this particular bar. *Well, maybe that explains why he was standing right next to the escape route and maybe wasn't looking all that hard for me.*

"Let's get out of here," she said. Knowing full well that he couldn't hear a word, she made exaggerated pointing gestures toward the door.

With the last beam of blue light evaporating across his arm, Dan emphatically pushed the bar door closed behind them. The instant the door was closed, they stood unmoving, still on the stoop, as an exhilaration of relief—to be outside, out of the blue light, out of the inescapable throb of long-forgotten music, out of the scene of utter desolate encroaching loneliness—washed over them.

Madeline said, "Oh, my God, I am so sorry," and laughed out loud.

There was something just a little goofy about him, the stoop of his shoulders, the enormity of his feet in the ultra-white gym shoes she later learned he had bought that day at Costco. A mortal after all. *Thank God, or he would be too impossibly good-looking.*

Madeline suggested they walk to a nearby place that she ardently wished she had remembered in the first place—a low-key homage to the '60s that still sold tie-dyed shirts, incense, and bumper stickers in a little shop adjoining the restaurant. It also boasted a lovely outdoor area, a giant screened-in porch strewn with twinkly lights that was heavenly on a summer night.

Though she was less than two miles from the house she had

lived in for nearly thirty years, she got lost. Damp with fretful sweat that grabbed at her mauve silk blouse, she surreptitiously scrutinized him for any sign of frustration aimed at her. They had met in person fewer than fifteen minutes before, so she had no cache of information that could tell her whether his appearance of good-natured reserve was just that, or if, perhaps, he had already decided that these two particular people, him and her, would not be seeing one another for much longer on the evening of September 2, 2012. Or ever again.

The remainder of the evening on that charming patio was a muddle of words and twinkling lights and perfect summer air, a moment when their hands met on the tabletop and did not let go, and the realization of the most magical, most hoped-for thing of all: that there is a pull, a force between one person and the person on the other side of the table, that is drawing the two of them together. Madeline could barely wait for the moment when their lips would meet.

Their hands remained locked as they walked to Dan's car. When his little SUV that was strikingly similar to her own pulled up in front of her house, Dan and Madeline dove toward one another in a passionate, feverish embrace. Madeline drew her head back and said, "I'm debating whether or not to invite you in."

"Then don't," said Dan. "Not if there's any hesitation whatsoever. Wait until there is none."

*Well, if this is a standard line he uses to charm the pants off women, I'll bet it works pretty damn well.*

Dan continued, “It will be magnificent. Whenever it happens. You must know that. You must be able to feel that, too.” He put the car in gear to signal his readiness to part.

“OK,” said Madeline. “All right.”

Halfway up the stairs to her front door, Madeline turned to give Dan a final wave. *Be here now—what does that mean? What am I supposed to be feeling?*

## Chapter 6

*Auggie* and Bess had known Madeline only as a single woman whose children were grown and gone. Madeline felt with them that she was Botticelli's Venus—a creature who had emerged from the sea, alone, a fully formed adult with no past whatsoever. Madeline was sometimes dizzy with the strange feeling this engendered, a lightness from the absence of history's weight.

Madeline had met Bess first—nearly four years prior—shortly before Bess and Auggie were even living together, let alone married. Madeline remembered the day she met Auggie. She recognized Bess's dog at the park with someone who wasn't Bess and realized this must be the Guy. She worked to contain her giddy exhilaration in front of Auggie, her joy to be witnessing the beginning of their beginning. Auggie and Bess served as Madeline's living hope chest. Their whirlwind romance and seemingly happy ending fueled Madeline when her own optimism was tattered or in flames.

"Now, exactly what is our role here, Madeline?" Auggie was

barely able to contain his delight. "What do you need from us—when this Dan person shows up?"

Madeline sat on one side of her dining room table across from Bess and Auggie. After the walk with Ellie, Madeline's renewed burst of energy for the prospect of Living in the Moment manifested itself in the form of shooting off a text to Dan: "Hey, no idea what you're up to this evening, but I'm having some friends over for dinner. Join us later if you're free. I made pie." He had texted back that he'd love to come by, but didn't want to infringe on her time with good friends. He suggested he could stop by around eight thirty.

"Auggie, you're being weird," Madeline said.

"No, no. I'm serious. We want to be there for you. We just need to know what our role is." Auggie radiated a decidedly boyish quality, in the best sense—he possessed untarnished enthusiasm and was completely lacking in guile. He also sported the exact same classic haircut that Madeline's brother wore throughout his Boy Scout years. Between Auggie's Buddy Holly horn-rims that were ever so slightly too large for his thin features and his unbridled exuberance for the task at hand, he was adorable. Bess nearly always found him adorable and made this obvious with frequent, glowing glances at him. Across the dinner table from Madeline, the two of them radiated goodwill and love. It delighted Madeline and made her misty and wistful and, as her son would have said when he was a little boy, sickenated.

Madeline rarely cooked any more and seldom sat in her

dining room to enjoy a meal. She felt strangely out of place in her own house and found herself wishing to grab onto the coattails of Auggie's high spirits.

Auggie continued: "I mean, are we chaperones here? Do you want us to stick around until after he leaves? We would love to do that for you." He put his arm around Bess and pulled her head over to lean against his own. "Wouldn't we, babe? Chaperones!"

"Like I said," Madeline interjected, "being weird, Augster. Very weird."

"Fine," Auggie said in mock pique. "Let's cover some basics, then. What does he look like?"

"Well, like an underwear model, according to my daughter-in-law. You know, the usual stuff: tall, intense blue eyes, wavy brown hair, luscious body. Did I mention luscious body?"

"Hold everything! Did I have the wrong idea here?" Auggie said. "Maybe you want us to leave right away! Maybe you're dying to be alone with him! Maybe the whole 'why don't you come over while I have friends here thing' is just a ruse to make it *seem* innocent." Bess could barely get her wine glass safely onto the table, she was giggling so hard.

"Auggie, seriously, don't do anything one bit differently than if Dan wasn't here. Really. Stay as long as you want to stay. Leave when you want to leave. Like always!"

"OK, OK. Understood. Back to some basics, then," Auggie said. "What does Dan do? He's not really an underwear model, is he?"

"Ha, no. He's retired, actually. As of two years ago. His company was being restructured, and he decided it was a good time to leave, rather than wade through the mess of all that. Meaning that he doesn't have to work. Ever again. Now he divides his year into quarters: late summer and fall in Chicago, winter in a village in Mexico, spring in Wales, where he lived for a long time, and summer exploring a new corner of the world every year. Oh, and he's younger than I am. Did I already mention that—that he's a little younger?"

Auggie stared at her. "So he's retired *and* he's younger *and* he's hot; am I getting this right?" He turned to Bess and said to her, "Honey, I'm just telling you right now, if it doesn't work out with Madeline and the underwear model, I call dibs."

"I just met him last night," Madeline said. "Way too soon to know if he's dibs-worthy. Let's see how the rest of the evening goes."

"Well, what about a sign then? Maybe we should come up with a sign—two signs—one if you think it's going well and you want us to leave so the two of you can be alone, and another if it's not going so well and you want us to stay."

"It really doesn't matter what I say, does it? You're deep into your own thing here. More pie, Auggie?"

"You betcha."

By the time Dan tumbleweeded through the front door and into the dining room, Auggie and Bess had pushed their chairs back from the table in healthy respect of keeping a certain distance from the remaining scrap heap of pie. Auggie and Bess looked Dan up and down while Dan looked the tumult of plates up and down, and before fifteen minutes of interesting conversational tidbits had crisscrossed the dining table, Auggie turned to his wife and said, "Well, honey, we really need to get going."

"What?" Madeline said, nearly before the words were fully out of Auggie's mouth. "Really!?"

"Really. Come on, babe." And with an incredible efficiency of movement, he grabbed Bess's hand, pulled her up from her chair, and led her toward the front door while both of them exclaimed the virtues of the food and the wine and the company, until the door shut behind them and their continued words drifted into the evening air. By the time Madeline took the ten or so steps back to sit at the dining room table, the atmosphere had shifted dramatically. The light-hearted ease had evaporated; in its place, a disquieting feeling hovered.

Dan gave a faint chuckle. "Nice folks."

"The best," Madeline replied.

Dan gazed at the table before him, laden with the evening's relics. As if he had read the crusted plates and crumbs like tea leaves, Dan said, "This house is so you. You are everywhere."

"Really?" Madeline retorted, more than a tad skeptically, as he had arrived less than a half hour before and had seen only two rooms. She shifted in her chair and folded her hands in her lap. "How's that?"

"It's so clear what this house is. It's the place that you created and have worked hard to protect," Dan said.

Madeline relaxed slightly in her chair. "Really?" she said again, her skepticism somewhat lessened and her curiosity stirred.

"It's a haven to encircle all of the people you love," Dan said.

Madeline thought: *Just how much longer do I have to wait to fuck this guy?* But what she said aloud was, "Huh."

"There is love everywhere," Dan said, still looking down at the plates.

*Maybe not quite yet,* she considered. *But soon. Very soon.* Madeline felt the blood rush to her cheeks from the thought. It thrilled her, yet also filled her with quiet apprehension. She said in a pitch that was tauter and higher than usual, "Would you like a house tour? Want to see the rest of the Haven of Love?"

Strolling the rooms, Dan remained decidedly quiet. Madeline ran her fingers along walls and gestured with giddy abandon as she dug up nuggets of historical facts about the 100-year-old house and recounted treasured memories of her thirty years within the confines of its walls. Dan nodded once or twice. He knit his brow now and again.

The house tour completed, Madeline plopped down beside Dan on the sofa, their thighs pressed together. The arc of the evening—the deep pleasure of Auggie and Bess, the astonishment of Dan actually *getting it* about her house, the chance to tell its stories—had left her in woozy, buoyant spirits. She sighed aloud and rested her head against Dan's shoulder. He reached his arm to encircle her, kneaded her shoulder, and then withdrew it.

"Are you feeling it? Are you as totally uncomfortable as I am?"

For a split second Madeline thought he must be pulling her leg—a bit of ha-ha, ironic humor—but one quick look at his face persuaded her that this was not the case. "What?" she said.

"You can't tell me you're not feeling the same. How completely different this is from last night. How awkward."

"No...I...I'm so sorry that you're feeling uncomfortable."

"Last night just flowed. Every minute. Flow." Dan sat forward on the couch, leaning as if ready to spring.

"You look like you're thinking pretty seriously about leaving," Madeline said.

"I am. Thinking about it. This is just so...weird. I'm not sure what I should do," Dan said.

Something old and very deep within Madeline felt a profound shame. She tamped down the instinct to apologize over and over, to do anything, to do everything, that might possibly make Dan feel better, want to stay, want to hold her, want her. She was also aware of a flash of rage, an intense desire to slap Dan's flow-spouting face. Inside a part of her screamed, *Fuck you, you arrogant fuck!* Alongside the shame and the blind anger, the most profound feeling of all was a wish that something, just one thing, could be simple. Clear. Easy. Known.

With swift and precise movement, Madeline pushed Dan backward on the couch, threw her leg across his lap so she fully straddled him, and gripped his head between her two hands. "Want to know what I think you should do?" Madeline moved in, her lips, tongue, teeth showing all of the threat, and all of the promise, of a wild and starving animal. She threw her head back. "Any questions?" she asked.

Taking Dan's hand, she led him to the staircase. With her back to him, Madeline ascended with measured, deliberate steps, resting their entangled fingers against her ass, with every intention that he pay keen attention to it. She took her time lighting the two candles on her bedside table, her back still to Dan, waiting for the match to burn all the way down before she blew the slightest puff of air. Standing behind her, Dan reached one hand out to caress her backside and took a step forward and cupped her breast with his other hand. They stood for a time, motionless, listening to one another's breathing—and that marked the last instant of anticipation, or of anything languorous. Madeline ground her buttocks into Dan's pelvis, hard, and rocked it from side to side. His fingers dug into the crotch of her jeans.

Clothing flew. Hands could not explore fast enough, could not cover enough ground. Lips, tongues, saliva were everywhere, all at once. The air in the room thickened to a fecund hothouse from the blossoming of body parts and ooze of fluids.

Dan gripped her haunches and pulled her onto him, astride him as she had been on the couch. Madeline ran her hand along his cock as she slid him inside her and shut her eyes tight to block out any thought, any hint of any sensation that was not the feeling of his cock reaching into her.

Dan seized her hand and enlaced his fingers with such force that Madeline's eyes snapped open. Her first inclination was to gasp. She had never seen a look quite like the one on his face. His impossibly blue eyes wide open, his body trembling, Dan looked right at her, right into her, with a hungry yearning that pronounced there would be no place for a single part of her to hide. A sound arose from deep in her gut, a sound she was not even sure was her own. And when that sound reached up through her body and spilled from her mouth, she was gone.

## *Chapter 7*

**Dan** slept through Madeline rising at her usual early hour. *The mark of a nomad that he can sleep so soundly in a stranger's bed,* she thought. Madeline considered waking Dan with a cup of coffee and a kiss, but she so treasured her morning routine that she elected not to. The blush of sex remained on her cheek from the night before as she made an extra-large pot of coffee and cleaned up the last few dishes from the dinner with Auggie and Bess. She sat down at her chair in the sun-drenched back room—the smallest room in the house, but her favorite. The little room jutted off the main house, and with windows on three sides it felt like being absorbed into the outdoors. Madeline opened the windows and breathed in the scents and sounds of her backyard.

When she had fully savored her first sips of coffee, Madeline opened her computer to read the news and check her mail.

*How cool Claire is writing from Asia,* was Madeline's first thought when she saw her daughter-in-law's name on the list of e-mails. In less than an instant, however, the rosy afterglow from the previous night cleared her head and she thought: *No, not cool at all. If Claire is e-mailing me from Asia, something's wrong. Really wrong.*

i'm sitting in a hostel in kuala lumpur and trying to reconcile the intensity of having stood in a river with my face resting against the temple of a young elephant's massive head and my hands lost in the playful curling of his trunk with the fact that all i can think about when i'm not engaged in an active pursuit of some kind or a conversation with someone new is that i'm a terrible person and should've gone to be with Savannah as soon as i knew she was pregnant... that i should've stayed in chicago two summers ago and fought for custody and maybe Savannah and my mom would both be so much better off for it... that i should've, should've, should've... i have not lived my life the way i've really needed to over the last three or four years. i love john and our marriage is something i want so desperately to protect, but i don't know how to be fair to him and our life and also be the person i need to be to be able to live with myself. i suppose i'm asking for your advice...as a friend, as a mother-in-law, as a professional woman. I don't know how i can go back to boston and stay there without Savannah. i don't know how john would get by without me. i've spent almost the entire time i've been gone stressing out about how not to spend money on anything unnecessary and listening to john's worries about how he has no money coming in in boston and i can't help thinking he just wouldn't be able to support himself without me working full-time. but john is a grown man with a massive line of credit and Savannah is my little sister who has no support or resources—how is this even a difficult decision? i need to be in chicago. how does a marriage like ours survive a year apart? will i only make things worse by being in chicago? is there any chance my mom will—no, there's no chance. i don't know, i don't know, i don't know. i'm on the verge of a nervous breakdown all the time. i'm terrified that when i get back i'm just going to fall apart completely. i'm terrified that john needs more from me than i have to give and that i need more from him than he has to give. what do i do?

## Chapter 8

**Madeline** was reading Claire's e-mail for the fourth time when she heard Dan's footsteps on the stairs. He was fully dressed, wide-awake, and seemed shy. He carried an ancient brown-paper grocery bag that, so far, was always his companion. He kissed the top of her head. "Madeline," he said, "I don't want to be presumptuous, but I'd really like to cook dinner for you, make you a whole feast. The presumptuous part is, I would have to do the cooking here. You know, because I'm bouncing between my brother's family and my sis while I'm in Chicago. Believe me, it would be tragically awkward to do it at either one of their houses.

"Any evening that you're free, if you agree," he added. "I have a special lentil dish that I learned from the Tamil family I told you about. It cooks all day long and makes the entire house smell like heaven."

Madeline was a bit stunned that this request was the first thing out of Dan's mouth. She didn't have a clear idea of what she had expected in the way of morning-after conversation, but this was not it. Claire's e-mail whirled inside her head. *I'm a terrible person...how does a marriage survive...will I make things worse...nervous breakdown...nervous breakdown... what do I do...what do I do.*

The only thing she could think to say was, "Are you always this wide-awake first thing in the morning? No coffee, even?"

"I've been awake for about an hour. Thinking. Remembering. Your sounds. The touch of your hand. Letting it all swirl around in my head while the morning sounds of your house drifted in."

"In case it's not obvious, this is me swooning."

It wasn't so much his words as his voice. His gentle, melodic tenor was a lullaby to Madeline. She wanted to lean into it, rest her head on it, let it embrace her and soothe her. When the sex was over, and the two of them lay in bed the night before, Dan had told her tales from his experiences in distant lands. How he had adopted a sort of personal mission to live *inside* widely varying sorts of lives, trying to put aside the accumulated fifty-year frame of reference and see with new eyes what the world could look like. She had been mesmerized. She became King Whatever-his-name-was to his Scheherazade as he recounted sumptuous details that made each story come thoroughly alive. She had moved her head from its resting place on his chest so the heady aroma of his skin and the rise and fall of his chest as he breathed and spoke would not distract her from his words.

Lying on his back with his head on the pillow, Dan had spoken upward into the night-dark room, as if his words were painting the ceiling with vivid scenes. Madeline lay with her head on her own pillow, also facing the ceiling, as if Dan's images were indeed coming to life there. But after a time, it was only his voice that she heard. The words ceased to have meaning. She listened as if it were music, grateful that Dan would not be able to see the tears forming at the corners of her eyes, moved as she was by the peacefulness she felt as she listened.

When Jeff moved out of the house and into his own apartment ten years previously, the first thing Madeline had done was buy a new bed. And, she had never liked the off-white curtains that had come with the house when they bought it—she swore they smelled faintly like mold and age and dust no matter how many times she washed them. She tossed them out, along with their discolored faux-brass hangers, and replaced them with bright white drapes that let the morning light show through. Madeline did some extra work and put the money aside to buy a new bureau for her clothes—a handmade, light-pine cabinet in the primitive style she loved. She changed everything in the bedroom, making it new and making it hers. Gone was the debris that trailed behind Jeff everywhere he went. She had transformed the room into a clean, inviting, warm oasis. And she had done it partly in anticipation for a moment like this one with Dan—so she could be transported, to a place where she had never been before.

"And I love coffee, by the way," Dan said. "One of the greatest pleasures in all of life. I just don't need it to wake up. All the better to be fully awake beforehand in order to drink in the richness of the experience."

"Words to live by," Madeline said, immediately regretting her naked attempt to rein in her swelling feelings via forced glibness.

"But I was serious about dinner. I want so much to cook for you."

"Oh, yes, absolutely. I adore it when someone cooks for me." This was actually a dramatic understatement; Madeline knew well that she was complete putty in the hands of anyone who prepared a meal for her, even a mediocre one.

"Good," Dan said, reaching into the inevitable grocery bag and pulling out two silver candlesticks. "Because I really want it to be special. I hoped you would say yes, so I borrowed these from my brother." For the second Madeline sat speechless, he reached into the magic bag again and retrieved two beeswax candles. "He didn't have any candles. I took a chance and got these myself."

"Wait a minute," Madeline said. "It seems like you must have been pretty confident that you'd end up spending the night here. Speaking of presumptuous." Her tone was ironic, but Madeline recognized that she was wandering in a heavy fog of romanticism and lust and knew that this hopefulness often led her to tamp down any creeping mistrust or suspicion.

"Confident?" Dan said. "Not at all. I can't predict the future; I can only sense the direction it seems meant to go."

Madeline reverted back to her swoon and paused for a second to catch her breath. "I got an e-mail this morning—from my daughter-in-law Claire, my son John's wife. She's in Kuala Lumpur. Her baby sister Savannah is pregnant. I know Claire.

I think the bottom line is that she is going to end up moving back here. To Chicago. Meaning: move in with me."

Dan pulled out a chair and sat down at the table across from Madeline. He scanned her face silently then put his hand atop hers. "Of course she is. She'll move back here because she knows who *you* are." Madeline let out a small snort. "Like I said last night: you are the person who has protected this haven. That's why I want to make this dinner *for you*. It's your turn to be cared for."

*Jesus,* thought Madeline, *can that possibly be true?*

## Chapter 9

***When*** Dan departed for his day's adventures, Madeline glanced at the silver candlesticks gracing her dining table and returned to her spot in the back room. The magnitude of Claire's e-mail message rolled through her like an unexpectedly muscular ocean wave.

*Savannah is pregnant. What in the world will this mean for John?*

Madeline and John had been unusually close well before Jeff moved out, but even more so afterward. When John left for college, Madeline was not sure how she would bear it. She lingered in his dorm room until John said, with gentle affection, "Just how much longer are we going to drag out this goodbye?" Madeline knew it was time for her and Kate to leave. She regarded her boy, who had become very much a man and a near carbon copy of his father. Handsome though, rather than cute. Strong and quiet, rather than a whirlwind of psychic energy. Madeline pulled the car over only once as they headed back to Chicago without John, sobbing wretchedly for a number of minutes at the side of the road. Kate later remarked, "Actually, you did way better than I thought you would."

John never wavered from his plan to return to Chicago after graduation, and four years after John gave Madeline one final, powerful goodbye hug in his freshman dorm room, she helped him move back to Chicago and into his first apartment. Of course Madeline had offered John the alternative of moving back into the house, but John was possessed of a great determination to stand on his own two feet.

Madeline knew she had gotten the great gift of time—she had been able to take years to gradually let go of the ferocious, iron grip of love that she carried for John. Her transition continued through John's first job. Being in one place for an eight-hour workday proved exceptionally difficult for John. He found both the lack of physical activity and the claustrophobia of a confined space challenging. Luckily for Madeline, he was therefore eager for any excuse to take a break and get out of the office, and she was happy to drive forty-five minutes each way for the chance to treat John to lunch.

For one of their planned outings, John had a new favorite place in mind, as he wanted to introduce his mother to her first oatmeal milkshake. The idea seemed wholly disgusting to Madeline, but John's enthusiasm for both the shake itself and the idea of acquainting his mother with this culinary marvel was palpable and infectious. But when her baby boy, now twenty-four years old, sat across the table from her with their oatmeal shakes before them, Madeline knew John well enough to see that some dark, agitated cloud had gathered around him.

Madeline opted for the gentle approach. She asked John general questions: how was work, how were things going with that one coworker, was his new roommate still drawing complicated maps from memory, etc. He answered mostly in the form of shrugs and nods while sipping his shake and taking bites of his sandwich.

John was always terse when he spoke, but never reticent or evasive. Lunch went on this way, with John uncharacteristically shuttered and Madeline stealing glances at him in an ongoing effort to decipher his runes. When the two of them were in the process of gathering up their lunch litter, Madeline decided to be direct. "You sure seem like something's up. Everything OK, John?"

John shrugged, stood up, and reached for his jacket. Madeline stood as well. Then John sat back down, threw his jacket across his knees, and curled the wrapper from his straw into a little ball.

"I just don't think she's into me," he said.

Madeline sat back down. "Do I have any idea what you're talking about?" Madeline asked.

"Didn't I tell you about this person I met? I told you! This amazing person?"

"Nope. Pretty sure I'd remember an amazing person story," Madeline said.

"The first time I saw her, she was...tearing into a chicken. A rotisserie chicken. Tearing into it with such...such...I don't know...gusto," John said.

"A rotisserie chicken," Madeline repeated.

"I've never seen anything like it."

"Gusto," Madeline repeated.

John and Claire married four months later.

And Madeline understood that from that point on, one of the very best things she could do for John, one of the very best ways to love her son, was to know and love his wife.

John had been married to Claire for nearly a year when Madeline met Claire's baby sister Savannah for the first time. It had been five years prior, when Savannah was ten years old and Claire was a newlywed of twenty-three. The sisters shared the same mother but had different fathers. Their respective fathers had done the bulk of raising the girls in different states—Claire in Illinois and Savannah in Arizona. When Savannah's parents divorced, the idea had been for Savannah to spend summers in Chicago living with her mother, Billie Rae, and also have the opportunity to visit with her big sister Claire. The execution of that idea varied a great deal from year to year, depending on Billie Rae's life during any particular summer.

The first time Madeline met Savannah, she was plunked in her sister's lap at the one and only public performance of John's old music group. Claire sat on the floor in the middle of the open room as the musicians set up, both arms bear-hugging Savannah as she rocked the little girl back and forth in exaggerated swings. And she was a little girl, too. Ten years old back then—but small for her age and small in general—she gave the impression of being a much younger child. She was all eyes—immense pools of deep blue that flashed out from behind chin-length brown hair that gave the very strong impression it wasn't going to follow anyone's orders no matter how hard they might try to maneuver that hair into place.

Savannah exuded scrappiness, just like her mother Billie and her sister Claire. Whether this was something they had learned because of everything life had thrown at them, or something rooted in their bones, it was certainly there. Savannah looked like she should be a literary character in a series of books that generations of children would adore, or the star of some adventurous, clever TV show.

Madeline didn't see Savannah again until the next summer. Savannah was not much taller, yet she still managed to show signs of gangly, awkward early adolescence, her arms and legs getting in her way all the time. Little, high-up breasts poked out from her T-shirt. Once in a while she could be caught with a far-off look on her face, as if she were gazing way, way into the future. Other times, she was a little girl; one of those legs would get in her way and she'd take a tumble and ask her mother to pick her up and comfort her.

Savannah didn't make her annual trip to visit her mother the next year.

The following summer, John and Claire lived with Madeline. John had decided to return to school in the fall, and he and Claire were upending their lives, and their deep love of their Chicago hometown, for John to pursue his dream of studying music. Madeline felt thrilled for him, thrilled at his courage and proud of his fortitude to direct his life toward an ardent aspiration. She also worried about every single thing: the strain on his new marriage, the huge financial burden of debt—as John would be taking on the financial onus himself. Madeline desperately wanted to help, but John wouldn't consider allowing her to help financially and the possibility was not realistically within her means. Madeline suggested he and Claire save their last few months' Chicago rent by moving into her home. Claire expressed clear relief at Madeline's offer. John, on the other hand, felt hesitant about the possibility that they might be taking advantage of his mother. But he put his reluctance aside and moved with his wife into his childhood home.

By then, it had been two full years since any of them had seen Savannah. When she arrived for her summer with her mother, she was thirteen years old. If she stood up straight as a die, she still did not reach five feet, but in those two years everything had changed. Instead of being all eyes and a hank of hair, she was all eyes…and absolutely *enormous* breasts. In an effort not to look like some cruel joke had situated a little girl's head atop a very-much grown woman's body, she had begun wearing makeup and coloring her long, still-wild hair.

Madeline felt, regrettably, that she had never known Savannah well and did not know quite what to make of her when she first arrived in Chicago that summer—whether she should talk to Savannah just the same as always or treat her like the entirely different creature that she looked to be. But other than spending sizable amounts of time trying to straighten out and generally tame her long mane, Savannah seemed like the same child as before.

At least that's what everybody in the family thought at first.

With Claire and John living in Madeline's house, Savannah spent more and more of her time there, and less and less time at her mother's place. Mostly she would sit on the sofa in Madeline's favorite room, watching hour after hour of TV shows about movie stars. Once in a while, she'd walk to the store a few blocks away to get herself a cold drink or a packet of gummy bears. Her favorite color was orange, followed by red, then yellow, then green. Madeline teased her, saying that they didn't have different flavors at all, just different colors. Then Savannah would make Madeline test her by giving her different colors with her eyes closed, and she would always make them out and then would say, "Ha ha, so there."

It seemed like every time she'd walk to the store, she'd come back home and spend even more time on her phone. She would sort of curl herself around it, like it was some precious, secret thing she was trying to protect, her eyes just a couple of inches from the little screen, thumbs flying, and her lips moving every so often.

Shortly after Savannah had become a regular fixture in the house, Madeline's daughter Kate arrived home for her summer break from school. Kate settled into her unchanged childhood bedroom, and John and Claire decided to move their bedroom to the third floor attic, so Savannah could take John's old bedroom as her own.

Madeline loved nothing so much as a house filled with family, and she drank up their very presence like a hungry cat with a bowl of fresh warm cream. The place was a damn mess. John set up a bike fix-it shop right in the middle of the living room. Claire cooked all sorts of bizarre-smelling concoctions at all hours of the day and night. The TV blared nonstop with Savannah's movie-star channels. Kate practiced her fiddle in whatever room happened to be empty. The household went for an entire summer without hearing those things that Madeline looked forward to the rest of the long year—the chirp of a cricket, the breezes ruffling the leaves on the ripe trees, the sounds of children playing long into the evening, all giving the sense that life does go on. It was the only drawback to a filled-up house. *Ah well,* Madeline thought, *next summer I'll be able to listen to all the damn crickets I want.*

Madeline acted for all the world like every wrench set on the living room floor, every pile of pots and pans, every gummy bear wrapper stuffed between couch cushions all were buried treasure. She got into the habit of doing everybody's laundry, insisting that it was just as easy to toss theirs in as long as she was doing her own, and it was way more efficient to do full loads, besides.

One afternoon, as Madeline was taking things out of the dryer, sorting, folding, and humming a medley of tunes from *West Side Story,* she screamed out, "Claire! Claire, come here! Claire!"

From the sound of Madeline's voice, Claire could not even imagine what catastrophe had come to pass. She raced down the stairs and into the laundry room, where Madeline held a pair of black lace panties in her hand like it was a dead rat that carried the plague.

"Are these yours?"

Claire laughed. "No. Definitely not."

"They aren't Kate's. I buy all of her underwear, so I can tell you this for a fact."

"You buy all of her underwear? *That's* weird." Claire took them in her hand and flipped them over, revealing that the back side of the panties laced up, top to bottom, with a flaming pink ribbon.

"Shit," said Claire.

"Claire, we gotta get that kid on birth control."

"Shit."

"Now. Right now, we have to."

Madeline's own words from two years prior rattled around in her brain.

*And now Savannah is pregnant.*

The lurid pink ribbon from the infamous panties formed a lighting bolt in Madeline's mind that she feared might rip through her brain.

*I fucking hate to be right sometimes.*

## Chapter 10

"*I might* have overbought," Dan said. He dropped a number of grocery bags onto Madeline's kitchen counters. "Particularly the lentils." He pulled out what Madeline estimated to be at least five or six pounds of lentils in three different colors. "But they won't go to waste. I make this dish a lot."

"No problem," Madeline replied. "There's plenty of room in the pantry."

Madeline was charmed when Dan shyly confessed a strong preference for being alone when cooking, and she was moved when he declared it to be a spiritual experience to deeply connect to nourishment made through his own hands.

Madeline soon discovered that when Dan cooked he carried on intermittent but extensive conversations with himself. At first she assumed that Dan must have been talking to her, as he spoke in his usual voice. But after saying, "What? What?" the first several times he spoke out, she realized that he was keeping his own company in animated fashion.

Dan had been right. The aroma that filled the house all afternoon was glorious.

She did wonder, however, exactly what Dan could possibly be doing to a pot of lentils that required a full day of preparation. She had decided not to mention to him that lentils were a favorite dish for her family. Both she and her children had made many different lentil dishes at many different times, and none of them took longer than an hour to prepare.

Still, when Dan lit the candles on the table and put the fragrant bowl of dinner in front of her, Madeline felt she must truly be in heaven.

"Tomorrow," Dan said, "let's get up early and drive to Michigan. To the dunes. I'd like to show you where I spent my summers. The leaves should be right at their peak."

*Yes,* Madeline thought, *heaven indeed.*

The next day, Dan chose a hiking trail that ran along a high ridgeline. They walked single file on a narrow path, with panoramic views—of the forest, the water, and the ridge—that fell away from their feet on both sides. Dan walked a bit ahead, and they were mostly silent as they looked back and forth drinking everything in. It was a warm day for the season, with the heavy, thick sunlight of late fall that Madeline loved. Dan was nearly at the top of the crest when he stopped walking and turned to face her. He smiled at her, and his blue eyes shone.

She breathed a little heavily from the climb through the sand. They stood a good twenty-five feet apart saying nothing. Dan looked a million miles into the distance, and then his attention was caught by something on the ground. He headed a little ways off the trail and into the thick undercoating of the forest floor, reaching down to pick up something. He walked over to Madeline and held out a long, thin striped feather.

"A feather!" Madeline said.

"A wild turkey feather," Dan said.

"Really? Are you sure?"

"Of course I'm sure. I grew up around here."

"I will keep it forever," Madeline said. "A souvenir."

"Of course you will," Dan said. Everything about his face disclosed the fact that he was beginning to love her and that this fact made him proud and shy and embarrassed and profoundly confused.

## Chapter 11

It was after 10 P.M. when Madeline's phone rang, and Claire's pixie-of-steel face flashed across her phone screen. "Madeline, you're not the first person I called. I've called everyone else I can think of. I can't reach anyone. No one." Claire took a breath and said, "I'm so sorry. I so didn't want to drag you in to all of this. I was so hoping my mom could hold it together just a little while longer. Just until I move back there."

When John and Claire tore themselves from Chicago and began their tenure in Boston, Claire hardly ever called. She apologized on a regular basis for being a lousy long-distance correspondent, feeling helpless as she watched all of her cherished Chicago connections elude her grasp, her own ardent desire to keep them close set against a paralysis at doing anything that might stop them from receding more and more into her corners. The instant Madeline saw Claire's face come up on her phone, she braced herself. *No way this can be good. No fucking way.*

"I don't know what's going on exactly," Claire said. "Savannah sent me a text yesterday saying that Mom was being weird, and now she texted me saying that she's pretty freaked out about how my mom's acting."

"Wait. Savannah is here now? Already? With your mom?" Madeline said.

"Yeah. I don't have time to get into all of it. Her father put her on a plane as soon as he found out that she's pregnant. 'You're-dead-to-me-and-you're-your-mother's problem'...that's pretty much the gist of what he said."

"Oh, shit," Madeline said.

"I think Savannah locked herself in the bathroom to text me. I think my mom's talking to Uncle Steve."

"Oh, shit."

"I know this is a lot to ask, but is there any way that you could go and pick her up? Bring her to your house? I'm so sorry."

"I'm working tonight," Madeline said, "until midnight. I'm on phone duty, so I can't leave. And Dan—that guy I'm seeing—isn't around. Let me think."

"Somehow she can't get any calls on her phone, so I can't actually talk to her. I'm piecing all of this together through texts."

"It's OK, Claire. If Savannah feels like she needs to get away from her mom—your mom—that's all that matters," Madeline said.

"I think she needs to get out of there now. Like, *now.* If I can get a ride for her, can she stay with you? Can she come up there? Tonight? Right now?"

"Of course," Madeline said.

"I might have to call a cab. I might have to see if I can charge a cab, if they'll take my credit card from here."

"What? That's insane. That's gonna be a fortune! I'll be off work at midnight…"

"Too much time. As long as I know it's OK for her to come up there, I gotta go. I gotta take care of this."

"It's fine."

"I'm so sorry."

"You're gonna really piss me off if you keep apologizing."

"Bye. Sorry."

At fifteen minutes after midnight, Madeline opened the door, and only then did the realization sink in that she had not seen Savannah in any form for two full years—since the Summer of the Panties—and that it had been four years since she had seen Savannah without a carefully and heavily painted face. Even the wildly striped hair did nothing to dilute the impact of seeing a child—a very small, very young, very sad, and very scared child—standing there. A child who happened to be seven months pregnant.

All Madeline could see in front of her was the giant-eyed little girl sitting in her big sister's lap the night they met, rocking crazily back and forth on the floor.

"Whoa, you're pregnant!" Madeline quipped gamely.

"Ha ha. You're hilarious."

"Look, you must be exhausted. We're not going to talk about anything tonight. Not a thing. You're going to get a good night's sleep. Your sister told me you can't make any phone calls from your phone, so I charged up my phone for you. Call anyone you want to. Are you hungry? Do you want something to eat?"

"I'm pretty tired."

"Want to just go to bed then?"

"Yeah. Well...do you have any milk? Not the weird organic stuff you used to get, just regular old milk?"

"I still swear you cannot tell the difference in the milk."

"That's what you always said about the gummy bears, so ha."

"I only have organic."

"Do you have chocolate I can put in it?"

"I do. Your sister left about a gallon of it when they moved."

"Can you make it for me? Can you warm it up?"

"Gawd, you're high maintenance."

"Can you bring it upstairs when it's ready? I gotta make a call."

"Sure. You go on up."

Halfway up the stairs, Savannah stopped for a second, turned part way around, and said very quietly, "Thank you, MadMad." *MadMad.* Madeline had forgotten that Savannah made up a nickname for her during the Summer of the Lace Underwear. The two of them had been sitting together on the couch in the back room—the only two people in the house right then. It just popped out of Savannah's mouth, "MadMad." It seemed to come out of absolutely nowhere. They had not been talking or joking about gummy bears or watching one of Savannah's crazy celebrity gossip shows.

"From now on," Savannah had said, "that's my name for you. I get to call you by a name that no one else in the world gets to use. It's just mine." Madeline was moved and tickled and deeply saddened by a little girl who needed so badly to feel special, in any goddamn small way she could.

When Savannah reached the top of the stairs and stood at the doorway of John's old room she called out to Madeline, "A lot of chocolate, OK, MadMad? Really a *lot*."

A thousand memories merged when Madeline heard, deep in a hard-won sleep, the sound of faint, small footsteps coming down the hallway toward her room. For many years John believed that his mother never slept a wink but instead lay there all night doing nothing more than pretending. How else to explain that by the time he reached her bedside—each and every time for his entire childhood—by the time he got close, she would say in a full, wide-awake voice, "What's wrong, honey?" Not a drop of sleep remained when Savannah whispered into the darkness, "MadMad. I'm really sorry. Claire said I had to wake you up. She's on the phone."

She took the receiver. "Madeline," Claire said, "my mother called the police. She reported Savannah as a runaway and that means you're harboring a runaway and that means you're gonna get arrested. The policeman is there with my mother right now. I have him on the phone. In my other ear. While I'm talking to you. You have to take Savannah home right now, or the police will come arrest you."

"You've gotta be fucking kidding," Madeline said. She ran

her tongue along her bottom lip, searching for a stray piece of chapped skin to nibble on.

"No. Most definitely not."

"Does this cop know about Uncle Steve? Does he know that Billie is talking to Uncle Steve?" Madeline asked.

"Yes. He knows."

"Does he know that Uncle Steve has been dead for fifteen years?"

"He knows."

"And this clown thinks it's totally OK to send Savannah back? With your mom? Who's having long conversations with a dead brother."

"You know how this works. She's not a danger to herself or others."

"Really. So how does he explain Savannah locking herself in the bathroom because she was so fucking scared?" Madeline bit through a flap of dead, dry skin on her lip. She could taste a tinge of salty-sweet blood.

"He's not a bad guy, Madeline. I've been talking to him for a while. He's been there with my mother for a really long time. There's no choice here. He's gotta do his job. Once my mom calls the police and reports Savannah gone, she's officially a runaway, and you are then harboring a runaway. He tells me this is a Class A misdemeanor. He tells me you could end up going to jail. For a year. So, you gotta take her home now or he sends the cops over to haul you off to jail."

"Fuck," Madeline said.

"Exactly."

"So he is totally convinced that your mom is OK? He is willing to put his ass on the line that a pregnant fifteen-year-old is gonna be safe with her?" Madeline asked.

"Yep. That's pretty much it."

"OK, tell you what, you get his name and his badge number, and you tell his ass that it's his decision and it's his ass. Put me on speaker phone if you want, and I'll tell him myself."

"Um, I'm pretty sure he heard you already. I got the other phone right here in my other ear. You have to take her home," Claire said. "Right now."

"Does she know all this? Is she OK with this? I mean…"

"She knows there's no choice," Claire said.

"Well, I'm *not* taking her home. I'll tell you what—if I am harboring a runaway and am very nearly a felon, I certainly should not be putting this kid in a car and driving her anywhere, right? And what's more, if Billie is in such great shape and is really OK and is actually ready to be a mom and not scare the shit out of her daughter in the middle of the fucking night, she can figure out a way to get here and get Savannah herself. Let's see her do that. We'll be waiting right here." Madeline ran her tongue along her lip once again, felt the little wound she had created herself, and searched for another piece of unruly lip that she could eradicate.

In a reversal of events from a half hour before, it was Madeline's turn to tread lightly down the hallway toward the blackness of the room where Savannah lay. She stood for a moment outside, but through the three-inch opening of the door, a little voice said from the nothingness, "It's OK, MadMad; I'm awake. I know..."

"I'm sorry, kiddo. Are you OK?"

"Yeah," Savannah said.

"Anything I can do?"

"No. It'll take them a while to get here. I'm gonna try to sleep."

"OK."

"OK."

"Then we'll make a plan. You're not leaving here unless you feel safe."

Madeline waited outside the door, but no answer came.

# Chapter 12

*Knowing* that sleep would elude her, Madeline stared at the dark ceiling and rolled Claire's words over in her mind: "She doesn't feel safe." Madeline's memory traveled once again to that summer two years ago—the summer that began with the richness of a house full of family and then disintegrated badly.

"She doesn't feel safe." Madeline had heard about the events of that summer's night from two years past the morning after it all happened. Madeline had awakened to then-thirteen-year-old Savannah curled up in a ball, deep in slumber on the couch in the very room where Claire told the story of the prior night as if it were a tale from very long ago and quite far away. Grotesque scenes involving Billie and Savannah, screaming sirens, spewed vitriol, handcuffs, jail, emergency protective orders, Claire being summoned, and a young girl—with a freshly stitched and gauze-wrapped gash across her forearm—now in the legal custody of Claire, with the legal residence of Madeline's home.

Madeline thought of a photo that Claire had pinned to the

wall of the room that she and John lived in that summer. An old photo of her mother, Billie Rae, when she was young—a grown woman, but still young. She was seated at a kitchen table, leaning forward in her chair to nestle herself, her slight-framed body, fully against the table. One shoulder tilted toward the camera in a way that looked both flirtatiously coy and thoroughly exhausted. The photo was not a close-up, and the distance made Billie seem even tinier...all long, dishwater blonde hair and big blue eyes. There was something else, too—a softness. The girl in the picture possessed a definite softness. This is what Madeline would try to remember. That there had been a time when Billie was soft. Vulnerable. Young. There was strength in that face. And fatigue. And pleading. Whatever came next, and next after that, Madeline would try to remember the girl in that picture.

## Chapter 13

*Growing* up, Billie Rae was the quiet one in her family—the youngest, and a good girl. She didn't give her parents any trouble, while her older sister Carol was raising hell with one boy after another, and her big brother Steve was puffing cigarettes and chugging beers and playing rock-and-roll music in every dimly lit, smoke-choked, sticky-floored, ear-splitting-feedback hole of a place that pretended to be some sort of a Big Deal. Like the horrible blue bar where Madeline first met Dan. The sorts of joints that litter the flat Midwestern landscape like mayfly carcasses around the middle of June.

Billie looked up to Carol and Steve like any younger sibling looked up to the sister who braided her hair and played schoolteacher and cleaned off her bloody knees and wiped her tears when their mother wasn't around. And the big brother who pretended he didn't know that Billie was tagging along behind him and would act all mad when he caught her. He'd put wriggly worms on her fishing hook and tickle her when she wrinkled up her nose. He would tease her that she was too scared to touch the fish except with one poked-out finger on its slimy, scaly belly. She would wail like she'd been stabbed. He would laugh and laugh but then give her a big squeeze.

She looked up to them like they were the be-all and end-all, and they pretty much raised her. Billie's father was mostly gone, keeping company elsewhere. Her mother spent long days shut up in her room and shuffled around her own house like a ghost...when she came out at all. Billie Rae was still too little to understand the yelling and fist-pounding that happened now and then. Once in a while, she'd hear the clatter of something being thrown or the terrible sound of a glass or plate breaking. She would pull the covers up around her ears and she would whisper into the darkness, "Angel of God, my Guardian dear, to whom God's love commits me here, ever this night be at my side, to light and guard, to rule and guide. Amen."

She didn't understand why all of a sudden, after a whole bout of hollering and stomping feet and loud wailing, her father was saying her big sister had to move away, had to go live with some "aunt" in Wisconsin who Billie Rae had never heard of. Billie stood by with her wide blue eyes while her sister threw her suitcase onto the bed and pitched articles of clothing into it like each and every one of them had done her unspeakable harm. Her sister paused every so often to wipe a steady stream of tears from her own face and from Billie's as well; then with a hug so hard she thought it would crush her bones, her big sister was gone.

She waited until the next time her mother came out of her room and Billie asked her when her big sister would be back. Her mother said, “Don’t you never mention her name to me again, Billie Rae. Do you understand me?”

Of course she didn’t understand. Billie returned from school every day and stood at the window so she could be sure she’d be the first one to catch a glimpse when her big sister came home. She knew from school where Wisconsin was and that it wasn’t too far away, being as it was the state right next-door to her own. She felt like her sister was close. Sometimes she felt like her sister was right there with her, and she swore she could feel her small, gentle hands running through her hair or hear her breathing in the empty bed next to her own. She would just wait.

None of us knows how our lives might have turned out entirely different save for one thing that turned us upside down.

It hadn’t been all that many days of Billie looking out the window and nights of her whispering her prayers in the bedroom she had all to herself. Her big brother did not come home one night. He wasn’t in Wisconsin, either. Billie understood he would never be coming home, or anywhere else, ever again.

Billie Rae was never quite the same after her brother Steve drove off the road that night. Billie herself never saw the old car sitting upside down with one wheel completely off and another turned on its side. She never saw Steve and didn’t have any way of knowing how smashed up he was, or if he maybe went peacefully without so much as a scratch on him. Still, the sound of car tires squealing, the crash of metal flying apart, and, most of all, the picture of her big brother with streams of blood running down his face haunted Billie's dreams for the rest of her days. Sometimes, when she wasn't even sleeping.

Billie Rae was twelve years old and in junior high school then. Her big sister was eighteen and a married woman. Once in a while Carol took the bus down from Wisconsin and spent the afternoon. She looked like someone who was trying hard to look grown up. Sometimes she took Billie to a movie or out for ice cream. She would brush Billie's hair and fix it in all kinds of fancy new styles. Carol would make Billie close her eyes, lead her over to the mirror, and then say, "Open your eyes! Why, just look at you, Billie Rae! I swear you are getting prettier every single minute."

Billie felt like her sister was making her play a game she didn't have any understanding of. She would get so excited when she knew Carol was coming, but she also ended up feeling confused and sad and like she had done something wrong. "When are you gonna come home?" Billie would say. "At least for a little longer? At least."

Carol would give a long sigh, partly like she was sad, but partly like she was mad, too. "I'm sorry, kiddo. You're on your own here now. You're just gonna have to do the best you can."

Carol would sigh again and look toward their mother's bedroom door. "Tell her I said goodbye, OK?" Then she would get all soft and touch Billie tenderly on her chin or stroke her hair a few more times. "You're my beautiful baby sister, Billie Rae."

She barely made a sound as she went out the front door and closed it behind her.

Billie went over to the mirror, trying to figure if she was beautiful like Carol said. She turned her head this way and that, checking the fancy hairdo Carol had pinned up from all different angles. "How lovely you look today, my dear," she said to her reflection, and burst into giggles. She ran to the bathroom and dug through a pile of things that had not been touched for many years, pawing and turning until she reached in and grabbed an old tube of coral-colored lipstick that belonged to her mama. Filled with boldness that came from her sister's visit, Billie plucked the top off and peered at the waxy crayon of color deep inside. She held the tube so close to her face while she slowly swiveled its bottom that her eyes crossed. Billie balanced her hips on the edge of the bathroom sink so she could lean way in, her toes dangling in the air, and drew a precise outline of her mouth. Patting her lips together like the stars she had seen on TV shows, she batted her eyes at the reflection that looked back at her and jumped down from the sink to stand back and admire her handiwork.

Billie pretended to take a couple puffs from an imaginary cigarette and, in a fake English accent, said "Really, darling, that new hair..."

She stopped in her tracks. Right there in the middle of that sentence. "Something's wrong," she muttered. "All wrong. I look all wrong."

Billie Rae unrolled a fistful of toilet paper and went to work feverishly on her painted lips, wiping and scrubbing at them over and over. Not even thinking or caring about the walloping she might get later on, she tore the lid off her mama's cold cream, thrust her fingers into the jar, and slapped a heap of the goo all around her mouth, scouring it with a fresh wad of toilet tissue. Looking back into the mirror, she let out a faint wail at what she saw.

Fetching a spanking-clean washcloth out of the hallway closet, Billie Rae covered her entire face with a thick daub of cold cream. She swiped at her face, rinsed the cloth in the cool running water, and swiped again until all trace of the cream was gone and her skin shone dewy and pink with little droplets of water beaded up and scattered across her forehead and cheeks.

Maybe something's wrong with the mirror, she thought. Maybe that's what was going on.

She fetched another clean cloth from the closet and the window cleaner from under the kitchen sink. She cleaned that silver glass with the tender care of one anointing a newborn baby, pausing after each polishing to look at herself again. Time passed. Evening fell. And still Billie Rae polished the glass.

"Steve," Billie said. "Something's wrong. My face doesn't look right. What should I do, Stevie?"

Billie Rae would brush her hair for hours. "That feels so nice," she said. "Please, just a few more minutes, Stevie, pretty please?" Steve wasn't ever the one who had brushed her hair —that was always Carol. But the one she'd gone fishing with and the one who made her special grilled cheese sandwiches just the exact way she liked them and the one who fixed her hair had all gotten mixed together inside of her. They were all people that used to be there, and now they weren't.

Billie was no longer scared to walk home from school by herself. She and Steve talked the entire way. He laughed and laughed at her stories. "You're still my baby sister, Billie Rae, but I swear that when your times comes, you are going to have yourself the pick of the litter, the cream of the crop. The boys are gonna be lining up, Billie girl, so they can laugh their fool heads off."

The door to her mama's bedroom was closed when Billie got home. Always. She knocked on the door, said, "Mama, I'm home? Did you have a good day, Mama?"

She no longer waited for a response.

It was completely silent on the other side of the bedroom door. Billie removed her shoes in the kitchen and tiptoed to her mother's bedroom. Without making a sound, she lowered herself onto the floor and rested an ear against the cool, glossy paint of the door. She sat for a long time, straining to hear even the faintest hint of stirring, an audible breath, any sign that there was a life on the other side.

After a while, Billie began to make up stories. Her mother had been secretly taken away by gypsies and was playing a tambourine with bright yellow and orange streamers every evening around a roaring campfire while men played the fiddle and women told tall tales and babies ran amok. Her mother had run away with a traveling circus and proved to have a remarkable talent with the elephants, who understood that she loved them dearly and would do whatever she wanted for the reward of her gentle strokes and soothing words. Her mama had been sucked right out of the window like Dorothy in *The Wizard of Oz* and was traveling through a magical and wonderful land, but all she wanted to do was get back home.

## Chapter 14

Still in Boston, Claire ended her double shift at the café with a heavy sigh. She knew she needed to face the task of planning her move back to Chicago and all the arduousness and craziness she anticipated would await her there. When she grabbed her phone, the icon announced nine voice messages.

"I saw this shit storm coming a mile away, I fucking did."

It was her mother's voice.

"You've always been out to ruin my life, always, and I can't for the life of me figure out why, you ungrateful little fuck."

"Savannah and I, we don't need your help. We don't need it at all, not one bit of your fucking, condescending bullshit like you are so much better than me and you have everything all figured out and we can't possibly get along for another second without you and without your help, and you are SO FULL OF SHIT it makes me sick."

"Don't move back here Claire. No one wants you here. Savannah doesn't want you here. I don't want you here. We are doing just fine on our own here, we are doing great, and she is having a healthy pregnancy and I am making sure that she takes good care of herself and I am taking care of her, and we have a PLAN and we're getting together a lot of things for the baby and NO ONE NEEDS YOUR FUCKING HELP like you are always so sure that we do, like we can't get along without you and your meddling fucking bullshit."

"Stay the fuck away from us, Claire."

The phone indicated a few moments' pause, then:

"Seriously, just leave us the fuck alone. Don't call us. Don't move back here."

And a final flurry:

"You are so full of shit. You have ruined, completely ruined, my life."

"We are doing GREAT. Savannah is doing GREAT. You lie about every single fucking thing, and you need to just LEAVE US THE FUCK ALONE. I was so happy before you ruined my life with your constant BULLSHIT and your lies, and everybody knows that when I cut Savannah's arm open it was an accident, a total accident, but you won't let anybody fucking forget about that, will you, you are determined to keep ruining my life and make me wonder what I ever did to deserve such a worthless, awful, mean daughter. A so-called daughter who keeps trying to knock me over and knock me down every time I get back on my feet and move forward and make good things happen for myself, you're right there, knocking me down. STAY OUT OF MY LIFE, Claire."

All was quiet for about twenty minutes, and then:

"STAY THE FUCK AWAY FROM ME."

## Chapter 15

After hearing the voice messages from her mother, Claire knew it was time. She needed to get herself from Boston to Chicago—immediately. Before the end of September, at least, giving her a full six weeks before Savannah's baby was due.

Claire called Madeline one morning. "I need your help," she said.

A single sentence, over the phone, and Madeline's pervading view of her daughter-in-law enveloped her. Any sliver of Claire—one word from her mouth, one sidelong glance if she were in the same room—and Madeline immediately felt like she was not doing enough. That she was bound to give out, fall short, run dry. That she would neglect to see something and botch something else. That there could be no such thing as "enough" help for the young woman who was Billie's older daughter—such was the ferocity of the desire to help and protect Claire that Madeline felt every minute.

Claire continued, "I have no memory of how to do this. I have no idea how people move from one place to another."

The decision that had begun with a gentle hand against a baby elephant's trunk in far-off Asia had been made. John would remain in Boston to finish school, and Claire would return to Chicago. She would move—once again—into the two rooms on the uppermost floor of Madeline's house, and she would await the gathering storm.

Billie Rae and Savannah had made it abundantly clear that this was thoroughly unnecessary, confounding, and, furthermore, insulting. They steadfastly maintained that they had full control of the situation at hand.

Unwanted in the new life ahead, and leaving her old life behind, Claire would await the gathering storm.

When the day of Claire's arrival in Chicago came, Madeline was reading in her favorite living room chair. She recognized the characteristic low rumble of a U-Haul truck when it pulled up in front of the house, though her back was turned to the windows facing the street. She considered how many times she had helped her children move in, or out, since each of them had first left home. Still, she rued the fact that at age fifty-seven she was able to do less and less; her legs now wobbled by the third flight of stairs, and she needed to put boxes down to rest for a moment all too often.

John and Claire had decided that Claire would bring the majority of their possessions back to Chicago with her, leaving John with a skeletal assortment of bare necessities as he focused on the grueling homestretch of school. Still, Madeline was taken aback when Claire lifted the U-Haul cargo door to reveal a truck crammed full, every possible square inch consumed in what amounted to a breathtaking feat of engineering. Reading Madeline's look on her face, Claire remarked, "Yeah. We had to pack it and repack it a few times."

Claire had also brought their dog. Everyone had marveled since the first day Claire chose the tiny, sleek brown puppy—who resembled a Dachshund that had been shrunk down to a mere four inches in length—that she had found the exact canine equivalent of herself. Proust was relentlessly demanding, deeply affectionate, possessed of strong and instantly formed impressions of all people and things, somewhat unpredictable, and generally in-your-face with his intense and abiding love.

Claire made four or five trips to and from the U-Haul and up and down the three flights of stairs for every one that Madeline made. Having endured two days of driving in a cramped and un-air-conditioned U-Haul, Proust was not about to leave Claire's side. He followed right at her heels—crossing the street to the truck, jumping into the incrementally growing empty space in the cargo area, wagging his mini tail as the women piled on each load, and yipping his high-pitched bark at random intervals—the entire time.

The U-Haul was emptied in an astonishingly short amount of time. Madeline stood in the street and gaped into the vast cavern of space as if it were a true miracle, as if an outline of the Virgin Mother would undoubtedly appear on a side wall, like Jesus on a piece of toast.

"I'll clean it out later," Claire said over her shoulder. "I want to do some unpacking."

"What are you talking about, clean it out? It looks pretty cleaned out to me."

Claire did not respond; she was already on her way into the house. Madeline followed, feeling as if a million thoughts trailed behind her.

Madeline leaned her head into the attic stairwell and called up to Claire, "Anything I can do to help?"

A distant voice, dimmed by mountain ranges of boxes and belongings that filled every bit of space between the two women, called back, "No. Thanks. I'll feel better if I can get a little bit done."

Madeline attempted to read and otherwise occupy herself despite the fact that it sounded as if elephants were tossing around large pieces of furniture two stories over her head. Every so often Proust let out a machine-gun burst of yipping, serving as Claire's impatient and insistent cheerleader and taskmaster.

Amidst the cacophony of chaos, Madeline found herself welling up with a strange wave of peacefulness. She wanted to talk with her daughter, and so she picked up the phone. Kate could hear the occasional yip, clunk, rumble, and clatter while she talked to her mother on the phone, and Madeline mentioned her wonder at her own surprising sense of peace.

"Ha," Kate said, "face it, Mom, this is your dream come true."

"What do you mean?" Madeline asked.

"The house is filling up again," Kate said.

When Madeline set down the phone, a ripe orange glow from the late September sunset flooded the room, and she noted a distinct lack of clatter coming from above. Again she climbed the stairs and leaned her head into the stairwell. "Claire? How's it going up there?"

"It's going OK. Come on up if you want."

Madeline slowed as she neared the top of the attic stairs, stopping a few steps from the top. Claire sat on an old wooden chair at a beloved kitchen hutch she had rescued long ago and had now transformed into a desk. She was leafing casually through a stack of papers when she looked over at Madeline and said, "What? I'm taking a break for a while."

Madeline had every expectation of utter catastrophe, but nothing could have prepared her for the scene she beheld. The sizable room looked as if a gifted and meticulous set designer had labored to create a masterwork from the following task: assemble a young woman's room that is both crowded and painstakingly decorated. Give prominent placement to her many hundreds of books, likewise to her artwork that has been collected from both friends and strangers since she was a child. Make clear that she is a lifelong denizen of thrift stores, where she has spent enormous amounts of time scanning the tossed-aside remnants of others' lives for objects that speak directly, and deeply, to her. Demonstrate that her aesthetic is completely idiosyncratic and fully formed. Fill all of the space. Make clear that each and every item in the room has a meaningful history and has been placed with great care.

Proust lay at the foot of the perfectly made bed, radiating serenity in a way that suggested he was always this calm and, furthermore, was prepared to chest bump anyone who hinted otherwise.

*The house* is *filling up again,* Madeline thought. She bit her lip to quell the flush of happy tears that filled her eyes.

# Chapter 16

*My mother hailed from a long line of rail-thin, nasal-voiced, energetic women who were capable and prepared at the drop of a hat to whisk into the kitchen and whip up a corn pudding or a batch of date bars well into their eighties and nineties.*

*My mother's own mother came from a family of five children —four sisters and one brother—Edna, Lula, Ralph, Nell, and Honey. Ralph was apparently a gentle and quiet soul who faded away and died quite young, leaving the four sisters to march into old age and beyond in their own brisk company.*

*Edna was the eldest, the smallest, the most serious, and arguably the most capable of the batch. The death of her husband in the early years of the twentieth century did not deter her from providing a loving home for their only son, while dipping her hand deep into the well of local politics and remaining involved in any number of civic organizations that endeavored to protect the excellent quality of life she found in Grove City, Pennsylvania. All the sisters had snow-white hair from an early age, yet they never seemed to change much otherwise. No one could believe it when one day, at age ninety-two, Edna registered mild annoyance at her son when he asked her for the correct spelling of a distant cousin's name—Becky—and she replied, "B-E-eck-eck-Y."*

*I was born in 1955 to a physician father and a homemaker mother who had earned a PhD in biochemistry. She worked as both a chemist and a physicist during World War II, helped write the first full assay of vitamin C, and then elected to stay home with her babies and never looked back. She committed to being a wife, mother, PTA member, churchgoer, bridge player, etc., with the square-jawed determination that I can only assume a woman would need in abundance to earn a PhD in a science in the late 1940s.*

*Just as Donna Reed, June Cleaver, and all the emblematic housewives of early 1960s television programs showed, women of this era lived their lives in dresses and skirts. In shirt-waist A-lines or slim pencils, they cooked, cleaned, chauffeured, reprimanded, volunteered, and—if they were especially efficient and read the right ladies' magazines—greeted their hard-working husbands at the door with a cheerful smile, a well-mixed cocktail, and the aroma of Big Meat wafting through the household. Women wore trousers only if the situation deemed this indignity inescapable. If it was blazing hot, it was acceptable to wear pedal pushers, a trouser also sometimes called clamdiggers, which were relegated mostly to Californians, bicycle riders, and teenagers dying to adopt new and shocking trends. Once in a great while the temperature and humidity would soar well beyond the pedal pushers zone, and my mother would unearth her shorts for an afternoon of gardening.*

*Despite the fact that skirts still hovered just below the knee back then, and pedal pushers hit at nearly the same place, shorts of the time were alarmingly, well, short. Though it happened two or three times each summer, I felt utterly unprepared for the sight of my mother dressed head to toe in clothes that never saw the light of day otherwise—white Keds sneakers, thin nylon ankle socks folded down in precise cuffs, extraordinarily short shorts, and sleeveless button-down blouses with jarring color combinations of checks and plaids.*

*I may as well come out and say it: the sight of my mother's mile-long, stick-thin, never-seen-a-drop-of-sun, otherwise-skirt-covered legs horrified me. I was humiliated and embarrassed and saddened well before the age that all daughters are horrified and embarrassed by their mothers. I immediately went about the business of planning an afternoon inside the house, safely behind closed, blackout drapes.*

*My mother gathered up her armament of tools with the precision of a scientist who had tested munitions during World War II. She inserted her hands into her cracked and worn leather garden gloves with the care and confidence of a surgeon. She approached an afternoon of gardening as her many generations of Naval-officer family members undoubtedly approached their duty to protect their country. And though I could not bear to look at my mother's frighteningly pale, spindly legs, I understood completely that when my mother returned to the house in the late afternoon—without a hair out of place or a drop of sweat on her brow—not a weed nor a withered stalk nor an unsightly rock would remain in the extensive garden borders. Not a one.*

*That's my heritage, the stock from whence I come. I will put on my gloves and I will get out there in that garden and I will take no prisoners and I will damn the torpedoes and I will full speed ahead.*

*My family is in need.*

## Chapter 17

*Every* member of the family had an irrational but intense distaste for Madeline's coffeemaker, but Claire's resentment and loathing reached an entirely different level. Claire's very first job had been in the coffeehouse directly across the street from her Chicago apartment, a place she had such a deep and abiding affection for that she still found any reason to drive past it more than a decade later. In the years since then, Claire had plied her breathtaking work ethic in a large number of cafés. She had babied and cajoled her fair share of finicky machinery in order to produce the sumptuously rich shots of espresso and foam flourishes that kept customers standing in line.

Claire would not go near Madeline's useless machine.

The coffeemaker had been a gift from a long-gone beau and held no particular sentimental place in Madeline's heart. Still, it was there. And Madeline had been raised by a woman who said, "I'm too Scotch to throw it away and get a new one" on a regular basis, though her mother had to explain this by telling Madeline an old joke: "What's the difference between a tightrope and a Scotsman? A tightrope occasionally gives." The moral of the message had stuck, despite Madeline considering the joke extremely odd and offensive and despite her mother having no Scottish ancestry whatsoever.

Each and every part of Madeline's coffeemaker required precise handling and placement—the handle of the filter basket needed to be facing forward; the lid of the basket assembly then had to be positioned just so; likewise, the lid of the coffeepot itself had to be screwed on to an exact point and then placed meticulously under the filter assembly. This struck Madeline as an apt metaphor for nearly all aspects of her life—that great effort and painstaking care were basic, inescapable requirements—and she never questioned the coffeemaker nor felt put upon in carrying out the steps each morning that resulted in an excellent and deeply satisfying pot of coffee. After all, wasn't it her own daughter who had said, "Not everything that's really hard is also good, but most things that are really good are also hard."

No one could ever figure out whether it was one specific thing or a compounding of smaller things that tipped the scales for the coffeepot. Every so often, the pot would simply refuse to allow the brewed coffee to flow smoothly into the carafe below and would erupt like a volcano instead, spewing a scalding muck of boiling water and coffee grounds across the entire kitchen counter and sending rivulets down the cabinet doors and dark streams across the floor. It had happened to everyone in the family at one time or another, and each family member had a unique response. It happened to Madeline only once. When it happened to Kate, she practiced putting the various parts and pieces together over and over and over, until she was certain that she had mastered it. But once satisfied that mastery had been achieved, she promptly forgot every step of the procedure and needed a refresher course each time she started anew.

John practiced benign avoidance. He managed to be someplace else, nearly always, when a pot of coffee needed to be made—partly because of the machine's unpredictability and partly because he so relished the cared-for feeling that came from someone placing a freshly made, wonderfully warm, aromatic cup in his hand. On the other hand, if elected, he held no rancor nor possessed any fear about the crusty old pot; he approached it with an even, calm attitude, expecting that everything would turn out just fine.

Claire gave it a very wide berth. She snarled at it and scowled in its direction when she went about the business of cooking. She preferred to not even pour herself a cup from a fully finished batch, so convinced was she that the diabolical device could not be trusted under any circumstances whatsoever and was, in fact, capable of genuine Evil.

Claire's distaste of the wicked pot was so great that she did not budge from her attic nest until she heard Madeline's feet hit the floor of her bedroom below at precisely 6:58 A.M. each day. Even then, Claire did not move a muscle until a safe period of time had passed, when she could descend the stairs with certainty that the morning's coffee had already been brewed and not by her—which Claire generally did not drink, although she usually agreed to let Madeline pour her a cup, noting the obvious pleasure it gave her mother-in-law. It was a dance the two of them did: Madeline got to make a loving gesture and Claire got to accept it with thankfulness and grace. But Madeline knew that Claire rarely drank coffee when she wasn't at work in a café.

Claire had long ago lost the ability to sleep in, and it was a challenge to remain upstairs awake each morning after years of managing the opening shifts in her coffeehouses. She awakened each morning sometime between four and five. But having her life spread out before her in one large room enabled her to accomplish a great deal in the hours before Madeline opened her eyes to the new day. By the time "good morning" passed from each to the other, Claire had read passages from a variety of books that recent events brought to mind; corresponded, both on paper and via e-mail, with people across the world who had stirred her soul into a permanent, unmovable, ferocious loyalty; written in her journal; scanned vintage anatomical drawings; continued the eternal process of organizing her thousands and thousands of photographs taken from world travels; jotted down ideas for a new children's book she was writing; and curled up in a corner of the room so she could manage a long, impassioned, whispered conversation with her husband in a voice so hushed that not even have the barest murmur would invade Madeline's dreams.

"I have so much I need to get done today." Claire squeezed herself into the small corner of the sofa that was closest to the door, as if the proximity to an exit and the sheer discomfort of her position would magically propel her to action. She cradled the cup of untouched coffee between her two hands and blew across the steaming surface.

With her idiosyncratic work hours and consequent erratic schedule, Claire alternated between two states that Madeline thought of as more or less "off," i.e., exhausted, and "on," i.e., energetic. In the "off" times, Claire walked with her eyes cast on the floor. She moved with such stealth that it was nearly impossible to know where she may be in the house, or if she was even there at all. She shrugged in response to any communication directed at her. She gave the ardent impression of wishing to be invisible—or perhaps to disappear entirely. During the "on" times, she could be stunningly talkative. The shifts came as a bit of a jolt to Madeline, when the same young woman who had slunk around in the deep shadows for a time suddenly plopped down on the sofa and became downright chatty, mustering an astonishing string of words, sentences, paragraphs, ideas that were not only exceptionally articulate, but were also delivered so blindingly, goddamn *fast* that Madeline had to concentrate especially hard on the content lest she get carried away by the spellbinding delivery itself.

Claire had an assortment of expressions that she peppered frequently through any and every subject she happened to be addressing, a trait Madeline found so utterly charming she watched for every new occurrence and was very nearly brought to tears by each of them. These included:

*at all whatsoever;*

*nonsense;*

*I mean, I feel like;*

*incomparable boob;*

*I mean, are you fucking kidding me?*

*ninnyhammer;*

and Madeline's personal favorite,

*conversational vortex.*

"Did you hear my big fight with John last night?" Claire asked.

"What? No!" Madeline responded.

"Nonsense. I can't believe you didn't hear it. I was seriously screaming at him. Because he was being a complete ninnyhammer, I mean, I feel like he started it because he was actually screaming into the phone at me, I don't even remember a time when he's yelled at me like that, ever before, when he was that mad and yelling so loud I actually had to hold the receiver away from my ear a couple of times, I mean, are you fucking kidding me? Seriously, Madeline, it's a little hard to believe you when you say that you didn't hear any of this."

"I seriously didn't. Are you OK? Is everything OK?"

"It's fine, it's fine. We talked again this morning. For a long time. That's why I'm running so late and I can't do this, I can't do this right now. I can't sit down on this spot on this couch and next thing I know some sort of thing has taken possession of me, hours of our lives have passed, and I realize that once again I have fallen into the conversational vortex that exists in this room! I do not have time for this today at all whatsoever." She paused. She shifted just slightly from her previous position of being bashed against the arm of the sofa.

"Possibly, it's already too late," Madeline said.

"Nonsense," said Claire.

## Chapter 18

*The* sound of the woman's voice was driving Madeline nuts. All singsong and la-la-la as she prattled on and on about how well things were going in every possible aspect of her entire life with no exceptions. Madeline tapped her fingers on the intensely varnished bar. She attempted to peel the label off of her beer bottle in little strips to spell out "H-E-L-P." Claire and her two friends—all sitting to Madeline's left—were deeply in the throes of some discussion that Madeline couldn't quite hear, their heads huddled together. The woman to Madeline's right talked on. Madeline didn't intend to eavesdrop. She would have strongly preferred not to do so. But the Bar Woman on the stool next to Madeline spoke at a volume that seemed meant for those around her to perk up their ears and marvel at her good fortune. Plus, every time Bar Woman made a particularly emphatic point, she would lean back dramatically on her barstool and squarely into Madeline's right arm. At which point she would wave her hand, as if shooing away a gnat. Madeline felt dangerously close. In a few short moments, she would no longer have a choice about it. If Dan didn't show up very, very soon, she was going to have to spin the crooning woman around on her barstool, slap her squarely in the face, and say, "Suffer a little, bitch!"

Dan had been visiting his sister for the past two nights, time together which generally consisted of him completing a laundry list of chores, repairs, and tasks that his sister had carefully compiled. This invariably necessitated driving around to an ungodly number of retail establishments known as big-box stores so they could gather materials, which Dan then used to build, fix, install, assemble, connect, secure, clean, tear down, buttress, erect, and, when all else was said and done, simply move from one location to another—and often back again if his sister decided the original arrangement had been better after all. Madeline had learned that for Dan most encounters with his family concluded with him going to the nearest convenience store, buying a six pack of beer, and tossing one of them down while he drove to his next destination. It drove Madeline crazy to think about it. Madeline calculated that it would take about an hour for Dan to get to the bar from his sister's house—she ran her tongue along her bottom lip and followed with her teeth, searching for skin to niggle.

Dan swooped in on Madeline—slumped over in creeping despair on her stool—as if he'd been lost and adrift for endless days at sea and Madeline was an emerald isle with Stella Artois running through her cascading stream-veins.

He swung her stool around and nuzzled his face into the crook of her neck, planting kiss after kiss. Enlacing the fingers of their two hands together, he bobbed his head, moved his hips and feet about, and performed a wild, giddy, drunken dance, all while ordering two beers—neither of which was for Madeline—the first of which he emptied in a single gulp. He grabbed the other bottle off the bar, lifted Madeline from her seat, and kissed her forehead between head bobs, dancing all the while.

Dan maintained an unflagging, feverish whirl of dance through the entire set of the band they had all come to hear. Claire and her two friends stayed at a measured distance, occasionally regarding Dan with the attitude of the stone-cold sober toward the merrily drunk—a mix of envy, pity, amusement, warmth, and disdain.

"Jesus, I missed you. That was the longest less-than-forty-eight hours of my life," Dan said as they were gathering their things to leave the bar. Madeline smiled, expecting to see a boozy glow when she looked over at him. But Dan seemed sweaty and slightly wild-eyed. "Really. All I could think of was how much I wanted to be with you." As the words came out of his mouth, Dan reached around the side of the bar and retrieved his inescapable shopping bag. But Madeline noticed there were two of them this time, and they were larger than his usual one.

"Ha," Madeline said, "looks like you did a little bit of shopping yourself, long as you were traipsing around with your sis."

"Huh? Oh. No. That's my stuff."

"What do you mean?"

"It's my stuff." He dropped the bags and enfolded Madeline in his arms. "I decided to stay in town longer. Till the end of the year. I can't imagine being anywhere else but here right now. With you."

Madeline realized that she was holding her breath.

"It's my stuff. I moved out of my brother's place. So instead of staying with my brother or sister and visiting you, I thought I'd stay with you and visit them."

*You're what?* Madeline thought. *You said what!* Madeline understood that Dan's current state of inebriation rendered any meaningful conversation impossible, which offered her a respite. The thoughts that flooded her head were so many and so varied; she would not have known what to say anyway.

Instead, Madeline told Dan that she needed to use the restroom before they left. She made a headlong dash into the tiny cubicle, bolted the door behind her, and grabbed her phone. "Ellie!" Madeline squawked into her phone. "Help! S-O-S! Assistance needed! Opinion required!"

Madeline did not need Ellie to be right in front of her in order to picture her knitted brow and slightly parted lips as she focused on Madeline's rapid-fire summary of the situation. And when Madeline said, "So, what do you think? Does this fall under the category of 'be here now'?" She knew Ellie would throw back her head and laugh to the sky, even before Ellie did just that.

"Phew," Ellie said. "OK, let me think about this. So you've told me that Dan's brother and sister both live here in Chicago, right? And you've also said that he always comes here in the summer or fall or whatever and bounces between the two of them, yes?"

"Yeah…," Madeline replied.

"So, is it wrong to assume that he will still be spending a fair amount of time with them? In which case, seems like it's mostly a matter of where he parks his crazy-ass, brown-paper bags. He's essentially going to be bouncing between three households, with you getting the honor of Keeper of the Bags. It's kind of charming. Also hilarious."

"I'm not feeling all that hilarious." Madeline worried at her lip to stem the tears. "Ellie, there is no telling what this next couple of months will look like. You know that."

"Yes, I do know that." Ellie's tone was suddenly somber. "I've known you for more than thirty years, Madeline, so I know that you are killing yourself taking care of everyone around you right now. Everyone. And there's way more of that to come. Why in the world would you not want some company for *you*? Whatever happens, if this guy can be there for you—for two months or two weeks or even at all—for God's sake, take him up on the offer."

Thus, with little fanfare and no discussion, Dan brought his worldly possessions to reside in the house with Madeline.

And even though Savannah was still officially living with her mother, she was liable to be at Madeline's house at any time—for a couple of hours or perhaps overnight—with or without Claire at home. Nearly eight months pregnant, Savannah had reached the stage where her belly looked conspicuously bigger each time Madeline saw her. When she was in the house, Madeline would generally find Savannah laying on the back couch, chewing crazy blue gum, and staring at her phone with her thumbs flying. Claire could generally be found in the kitchen, stirring odd admixtures made from potatoes and garlic. Claire was just hoping her baby sister (and her coming nephew) would get some decent food into them. When Claire and Savannah were both at Madeline's, Madeline and Dan stayed mostly upstairs. For Madeline, Savannah's belly loomed very large. Madeline had begun to feel awkward when she was around the sisters, a sense that *she* was encroaching on *them*. She was grateful for Dan's presence at these times, grateful for the moments he pulled her attention from the looming belly, grateful for a natural excuse to retreat to her room and loll around on the bed. They often read aloud to one another—poetry, usually.

Dan was partway through one of Pablo Neruda's love sonnets when Madeline sat up as if a shock had run through her. "Oh my God," she said, "I'll be right back."

Madeline remembered something she felt sure must be in a closet somewhere, a leftover from John and Kate's serious backpacking days. When she located it, tangled up with a rat's nest of cords and miscellanea, she was thrilled. She ran back into the bedroom and said to Dan, "Take off your clothes and get under the covers. All the way under, head included. And close your eyes. You have to close your eyes."

Dan obeyed her request without a word. When Madeline said, "Open your eyes," Dan found himself in darkness but felt a warmth that suggested Madeline lay near. With a small clicking sound, Dan saw Madeline, naked, under the covers with him. She sat cross-legged, so the top of her head held up the blankets and created a tent-cocoon, a private refuge lit softly by a headlamp flashlight that shone from Madeline's forehead. "Now," Madeline said, "start the sonnet again."

"Madeline, creator of worlds," Dan said.

"Why, sir, how you do flatter a girl," she said.

"A bruja. Truly, you are a bruja."

"Bruja?" Madeline said. "Doesn't that mean witch?"

"Yes, but more like an enchantress. A woman with the magical power to entrance. The kind of woman who can create worlds."

"Ah, well, I guess I can live with that."

## Chapter 19

*October* settled into a rhythm that struck Madeline as both lovely and bizarre. Between her two jobs, Claire nearly always left the house early in the morning and was gone until late afternoon. Madeline and Dan drank their coffee together each morning, had their breakfast, and talked about everything under the sun. Dan loved to borrow the neighbor's dog, walk to the lake, and then scour the beach for a good stick. Once he found a solid, hefty one that met with his satisfaction, he threw it way out into the water for the indefatigable Labrador retriever to fetch, again and again. An unusually warm October followed a blazing hot Chicago summer, so Lake Michigan remained preternaturally warm and still swimmable. Many mornings one or both of them might venture into the water with the dog or wade lazily along the shore. The breezeless, Indian summer mornings rendered the lake into a sheet of glass, a mirror for the enflamed trees of midfall. With no waves and no ripples of surf, the only sounds were the occasional wail of a gull and the gentle splash of the dog's paws as he swam to and from the shore.

When it was time for Madeline to go to work, Dan generally headed for the far south of the city, the neighborhood where he had spent his childhood. He had a favorite spot where he could do a long swim in the lake, enjoy an outstanding view of the skyline to the north, and pass time conversing with whomever else happened to be hanging out at the same spot that day.

Sometimes he would arrive back at the house before Claire; other times, Claire would be well into her four P.M. cooking when he returned. With Dan having swum and sunned and chatted, and Claire having been up and working since before daylight, an atmosphere of unhurried calm permeated the air Madeline entered when her own workday was complete.

Those late afternoons were cherished times. Madeline and Dan would sit together on the couch and look out the back windows. Dan caressed her fingers. She smiled easily. Time moved slowly. They talked about their day—Dan recounting bits of conversations he had with fellow swimmers or things he had read and Madeline sharing stories from work. They watched the birds or noted how the squirrels' movements seemed a bit more urgent with each passing day. Claire would join them when her potato dish of the day was ready, sitting beside the two of them on the sofa, the three of them lined up in a row.

Their conversations ranged from the sublime:

"It's funny you should mention *To Kill a Mockingbird,*" Dan said. "I always thought of my father as Atticus Finch. His seemingly easy way of just…doing the right thing. You could never see his wheels turning, but you knew that they were. That he was thinking hard about *right*."

...To the ridiculous:

"Has Savannah thought about whether she's gonna have the baby circumcised? Because she knows it's a boy. They're going to ask her that right away. In the hospital," Madeline said.

"Yeah. She already decided that," Claire answered. "She is gonna have that done." A few seconds later, Claire said, "I'm not sure I want to know, but what does that mean exactly?"

"It means they cut the fold of skin that fits over the end of a boy's penis. It's sort of an extra layer of...skin. When they cut it off, well, that's when penises have that mushroom cap look to them," Madeline said.

"Huh," said Claire.

"The whole thing has been a big debate. For years. About whether it's necessary. Which is why John's not circumcised. I couldn't see taking a scalpel to a brand-new baby without really, really good reason."

"Yeah, I can see that...wait...what? What? John's not circumcised?" Claire said, with wonder in her voice.

"Oh my God, did you just say that? We're talking about your husband," Madeline said. "Of four years!"

"I know, I know!" Claire laughed.

"Have you ever actually seen him...naked?" Madeline asked.

"I have! I have!" Claire leapt to her feet. "I just didn't realize that what I was looking at was...*uncircumcised*."

Dan opened his mouth to make a comment but thought

better of it apparently, because he closed his mouth again and let his eyes fall to his own lap.

"I gotta call John!" Claire said. "I gotta call him *now*."

"This won't be news to him, Claire. He already knows he's uncircumcised."

*What a strange thing this is,* Madeline thought to herself, *this time of my life where the two people that I am closest to are my daughter-in-law and a man I didn't even know two months ago.*

Around this same time, Madeline began having a recurring dream. The details were somewhat different each time, but the premise remained the same. It was an undetermined number of years in the future. Madeline had sold the house. A boisterous family with three school-aged children had moved in and made it their own. Madeline was no longer the Keeper of the Trains, and, as it turned out, this felt fine.

From that point on, the details of each dream varied, but Madeline learned, via the grapevine network of neighbors and friends, that the new owners had discovered something that was wrong with the house—something major. When she learned this, Madeline became fraught with guilt and worry that it was due to some horrible neglect on her part, something she had failed to notice of, take care of, fix, make right. And her failure to notice and to act had resulted in catastrophe. Disaster that was entirely her fault.

## Chapter 20

*I* **was** *five years old when my dog Heidi went into heat for the second time. My parents arranged to have her spend a number of days with the breeders where we got her. They had selected a mate for her. We all drove out to drop her off. The house lay at the fringes of land that were well past the suburbs, but not quite rural. There seemed to be dogs everywhere, some in large cages set around the enormous yard and others who roamed the house freely. I wondered if the same dogs always got to live inside, or if the breeders rotated them inside and out, following some schedule. Their immense pride in their dogs was evident. Both the man and the woman went on at length, telling me each dog's name and several of the dog's dominant character traits. I got the feeling that I was actually supposed to remember all this, because of their joy and the weight they gave to every detail they imparted.*

*It was a confusing mess to me, despite the good cheer. I wanted to know if Heidi would have to be outside in one of the cages, and I was told that she would, because she and her new male friend would need privacy and time to get to know one another.*

I could not understand the convivial good spirits everybody seemed to share. We were abandoning Heidi with strangers who were going to make her live outside all the time.

The body of a female dog makes a complete puppy from the original fertilized cell in about sixty-three days. The average size of a litter is usually five to six puppies, although the variation among dogs is enormous. It's rare to have just one puppy in a litter, but it does happen. A couple of months after we fetched Heidi from her exile, my parents got the wooden pen ready for her in the basement. The same old blue bedspread and dingy pink blanket that her first litter had been born onto lay on the floor. Heidi occasionally scratched at the blankets, rearranged them with her nose and paws, and circled around and around as she waited.

One afternoon, Heidi squatted down in a corner of the pen and stayed in the same position, motionless, and stared straight ahead. She looked like she was trying very hard to poop. I wanted to ask my mother if this was true, but she had already told me that I needed to stay completely quiet if I was going to watch. Heidi let out a long, low moan. She inched her rear end closer to the floor, so slowly, and out came a translucent thick balloon with a puppy inside of it.

There was only one puppy, which was an enormous surprise. My parents decided that we should keep her and that she should be named "Elf," the German word for eleven. She was to be the eleventh dog that my family had owned, if they counted a dog called Toby that my father's nurse had gotten for us, unannounced. We would visit him where he was chained at the far *end of our backyard until my mother couldn't stand it for another minute. I'm not really sure what happened to Toby. They also counted the black puppies from Heidi's first litter, even though they had died.*

*I don't think my parents realized that Heidi had been a relatively compliant, trainable dog until Elf. Looking back, I think Elf was mostly just dumb as a box of rocks. Even in photographs, she had a wild, glassy look in her eye—an animal with unbridled enthusiasm, absolutely no comprehension, the brute strength of an ox, the stubbornness of a mule, and a bad, bad case of ADD.*

*I thought having two dogs was great fun.*

*My grandmother (the good one) was visiting us, and my mother had planned a big dinner. An eight-pound beef roast sat on our kitchen counter, thawing out for the upcoming feast. My grandmother heard a commotion and entered the kitchen to find Elf with the giant slab of meat clenched firmly in her jaws. My grandmother shouted, "No, no, no," and reached out with both hands to rescue the meat. Elf snapped at her. My grandmother called out for my mother, who came running into the kitchen and immediately understood the situation. My mother spoke firmly to the dog and reached for the roast. Elf snapped at my mother as well.*

*I didn't see any of this. I came in at the part where my mother told me that my grandmother was going to be in charge for a little while and that she would be back soon. She put Elf on a leash and left. When my mother returned, Elf was not with her.*

*The only thing that was ever said about it was this: "I will not have a dog that snaps at its owner."*

*We sat around the dinner table that night as if nothing out of the ordinary had happened, though my father seemed unusually quiet.*

*I understood that we were not supposed to talk about it, but I was sick with sadness and confusion. I remembered the time when Elf was brand new, her eyes still closed tight, her body squat and furrowed with newborn puppy wrinkles. I was sitting inside the pen holding Elf on my lap—which I would do for hours and hours, filled with love and amazement at her every twitch and movement—but somehow she slipped off my lap this time. I picked her up, horrified at my clumsiness, and saw a tiny bubble of blood at the side of her nose.*

*After dinner the night when Elf vanished, after my mother had finished the dishes and turned off the kitchen light, I said, "Mommy, do you think it's all my fault? Do you think Elf was such a bad dog because of the time that I dropped her when she was a tiny puppy?"*

*"Maybe," my mother said. "Maybe it is your fault."*

## Chapter 21

"That was when you taught me about sex, Claire, remember?" Those words had just emerged from Savannah's mouth as Madeline entered the room. Savannah laughed a hearty, open-mouthed laugh. Her great round belly bounced up and down, requiring her to rearrange it. "We were just talking about the time Claire told me all about S-E-X. Don't you remember, Claire?"

"I have no idea what you're talking about. This is nonsense," Claire countered.

"No. It's true. We'd been waiting for Mom for so long, remember? It was, like, hours and hours," Savannah said.

"Waiting for her where?" Madeline asked.

"At the casino," Claire said.

"What do you mean at the casino?" Madeline asked.

"Well, wait, let's get back to the story here," Savannah said. "I can't believe you don't remember this, Claire. We were sitting on the curb, 'cause we'd already played in the car and taken turns playing taxi driver. And then you went through your purse trying to find all the little crayon stubs, and you let me draw pictures on the little scraps of paper you picked off the floor of the car and found in the glove box, and you made up a story about every picture, and still we were waiting. So we went outside and sat on the curb and you had me drawing pictures using just my toes in the dirt and you'd guess what they were. And you were being silly and making me laugh, guessing that the pictures were crazy things like a bunch of angels gathered around a brand-new baby elephant singing lullabies so it could sleep through the roars of the angry lions. I mean, I drew something like a circle and that's what you'd guess."

"Angels singing to a baby elephant?" Madeline arched her brow.

"Whatever. Shut up," Savannah said. "We'd been waiting *such* a long time. It was dark already. I just remember being so sleepy, like woozy, you know? And then I said, 'Claire, this girl in my school said her older sister is gonna have a baby. So my friend asked her sister where the baby came from, and her sister said that the husband stuck his wee-wee inside of her and went pee-pee and that's where the baby came from.' And I said, 'Is that true, Claire? Is that where babies come from? Is that where *I* came from?' And you said, I swear to God you said, 'Well, that's close enough.'" Savannah wrinkled up her nose and laughed loud.

"Nonsense," Claire said. "Never happened."

"Oh my God, you're the worst," Savannah said, picking up the sofa pillow and tossing it at her sister. Both of them burst into unfettered laughter.

"That's what I thought for *years*, Claire. Years!"

"You were a little kid! What was I supposed to say?" Claire said.

"Like, how old?" Madeline asked, biting into her lip.

"I don't know," Claire considered. "Probably four or five by then. This kind of went on for a long time."

"This *what* went on for a long time?" Madeline asked.

"We'd be out running errands—my mother and Savannah and me—or getting food, or whatever, and my mother would just sort of...drive over to the casino and say that she'd be right back. And she'd leave us there. In the car."

Claire's tone was strangely untroubled, but her voice became softer. She shrugged one shoulder. "She was basically bringing me along to watch after Savannah. Savannah was pretty little when this started."

"Little...like how little?" Madeline asked, ripping off a sizeable piece of skin that she'd caught between her upper and lower incisors.

"Oh, one and a half? At least one," Claire said.

"You were taking care of a baby inside of a car in the parking lot of a casino? By yourself?" Madeline felt decidedly alarmed, but the breezy nonchalance of the sisters made Madeline feel like a judgmental Church Lady raining on someone else's happy parade.

"Uh-huh," said Claire.

"It was fun!" Savannah said. "Claire made it really fun."

"How long would she be gone? In the casino?" Madeline asked.

"Sometimes not very long. You know, an hour. Sometimes

pretty long. That time Savannah's remembering is probably the longest. I think my mom drove us there right after I made lunch. It was dark when we left."

Savannah laughed. "It's all your fault, Claire," she pointed to her enormous belly. "You ruined me with that story."

"What did I miss? Somebody bring me up to speed." Dan poked his head around the corner, holding a rewarmed bowl of his lentils. Between the noise of the microwave and his animated conversation with himself, he had not heard a word.

Three heads turned in his direction. No one spoke.

"Wow," Dan said. "Must have been good."

## Chapter 22

Madeline didn't think about Jeff as often as she used to, which struck her as both remarkable and triumphant. But when she did think of him, she often thought of his "boomerang."

She had long heard the giggles and rumors from the mutual friends who ultimately introduced the two of them one evening. She and Jeff saw each other every day for two weeks after that, their words gradually becoming chicken scratch, background noise, to a deepening, captivated spell that took hold of them both. Still, in their demure newness, she took the first shower—separately—then waited while he took his. When the sound of the running water ceased, Madeline was unable to wait a second longer.

She opened the bathroom door to an entirely pink-tiled world heavy with steam. Jeff drew back the shower curtain, wiping the water from his eyes, and opened his arms to her.

When she pulled back from their embrace and took his hand to lead him to her bed, there it was. Her eyes widened. "It's my boomerang," Jeff said.

"Because it always comes back to you? No matter where it's been?" she said.

Jeff laughed. "No. Because that's what I call it."

The dazzling sun of the summer afternoon dimmed to dusk and then to dark before Madeline and Jeff uttered their next words. "So. Boomerang. Pleased to make your acquaintance."

Jeff laughed and kissed her on the temple. "It got broken."

"Oh, stop. That's not possible."

"Obviously it is. Possible."

It was many years before the Internet. Many years before Madeline was able to type the words "broken penis" into the Google search bar and get the following from the Mayo Clinic website:

*Is it possible to fracture your penis?*

Answer from Landon Trost, MD

Yes. Although rare, penis fracture can occur when there is trauma to an erect penis.

During an erection, the penis is engorged with blood. If an engorged penis is bent suddenly or forcefully, the trauma can rupture the lining of one of the two cylinders in the penis (corpus cavernosum) responsible for erections—resulting in a penis fracture. The trauma most often occurs after accidental injury during intercourse, but can also occur due to aggressive masturbation or taqaandan, a cultural practice in which the top of an erect penis is forcefully bent.

A penis fracture is a painful injury. Signs might include a cracking sound, immediate loss of the erection, or the development of dark bruising of the penis due to blood escaping the cylinder. Sometimes the tube that drains urine from the body (urethra) is damaged as well, and blood might be visible at the urinary opening of the penis.

A penis fracture requires urgent medical attention. The injury can usually be diagnosed with a physical exam, and prompt surgical repair is typically recommended.

Left untreated, a penis fracture might result in deformity of the penis or the permanent inability to get or keep an erection firm enough for sex (erectile dysfunction).

At the time, however, Madeline only knew what she had seen. And experienced.

"Does it hurt?" she asked. "Do I need to worry about hurting you?"

"Not at all," he said.

She giggled and then said, "I'm sorry to laugh. You *broke* your *penis!*"

"It wasn't so funny when it happened. It hurt like a mother. And I heard it break."

"You're kidding?" Madeline said. "What in the world happened?" Jeff took a breath in preparation to answer, but Madeline took her index finger and held it to his lips. "No, wait. Don't tell me. No history. Not right now. Just this moment. Just the two of us. And, of course, Boomerang."

Madeline became passionately attached to Jeff's body. She scanned its surface for changes to memorize. She took note of differing thicknesses of the hairs comprising his beard, ran her fingers along the crevasses of scars from a bad car accident, studied the calluses on each of his fingers from years of playing guitar. It took Madeline a very long time, a great number of years after Jeff left, to even consider being in the same room with a naked man's body that did not have a boomerang. She couldn't bear the thought. On top of all else, this seemed too much of a loss to bear.

When Jeff rounded the corner of his forty-fifth birthday and headed toward fifty, things didn't work in quite the same way. Madeline thought nothing of it, taking it as an early harbinger of their standing at the entryway of a contented golden old age, where they would laugh deeply and often, hold hands in quiet moments, and bask in the blessings of their life's labors. She was charmed by Boomerang's sometimes-softer edges.

Jeff did not feel the same.

"Well, honey," Madeline said to him, "you remember what we read. On the Internet. This could be a result of the break."

"Not after all this time," Jeff insisted.

"But, it was the Mayo Clinic, remember? It said—"

"Not after all this time," Jeff repeated.

Days, weeks, months, years passed. Other than Boomerang, the remainder of Jeff grew harder around his edges. He came to believe it *was* a harbinger—a herald announcing that their time together, the marriage of their intermingled souls, had come to an end. He believed that his boomerang was speaking to him, telling him this.

Madeline thought of Savannah, with her bright blue gum

and wide child eyes. She thought of her having sex, at the age of fourteen, with a boy she liked. A boy that turned out to be the father of her child. A boy whose body she would never come to know well enough for the smells and contours and gradations of pleasure to become a part of herself. A body that would *remain* a part of her, and of her son.

*What in the world had their sex been like,* Madeline wondered. *Did Savannah like it? Did she even want it?* Madeline hoped that she had at least made a decision that she *wanted* to have sex. For herself. Not because she was pushed. Not because she had no idea how else to keep a boy around. Not because she had been tossed around her whole life and had no idea what it meant to be loved, really loved. Or even wanted.

## Chapter 23

**Savannah** lounged around on the couch most of the time she was there, her belly getting so swollen that it no longer looked like it could possibly belong to the rest of her body. She wore a raggedy old pair of sweatpants that she borrowed from Madeline, a T-shirt she borrowed from Claire, and a giant sweatshirt she unearthed from John's pile of left-behind clothes from years ago. That girl dearly loved to wear everybody else's clothes.

The television chattered, as it always did, with Savannah not really looking at it. She mostly liked to push the remote control buttons every so often, make the sound go up or down, or switch to a different channel she would also not watch—and then go right back to pushing the buttons on her phone.

Savannah held the phone to her ear and said, "Daddy? Hi. Hey, what do you think I should have for lunch?"

*Oh my god,* Madeline thought, *you've got to be fucking kidding me. Not this food thing again.*

"Cereal. I had a big bowl of cereal for breakfast.

*Pause.*

"No. I only like creamy peanut butter, and right now all we've got is the crunchy kind. I hate that stuff. Plus I only really like peanut butter with marshmallow fluff, and pretty sure we don't have any of that either. What else?

*Pause.*

"No, I've had bagels every day 'cause Claire always brings them home. Plus that's what you said yesterday. What else?"

Madeline brought the big basket of clean laundry and sat herself at the far end of the sofa to fold it while Savannah carried on with her phone call. Savannah put her teeny feet in Madeline's lap. The littleness of Savannah's feet, the childlike tone of her voice—Madeline was not sure exactly what it was—but in her mind, she found herself sitting on that same couch, years earlier, watching her daughter Kate. When Kate was four and five there was a period when she would watch the same movie over and over again...and then watch it some more after that. *My God,* Madeline thought, *Kate would have been the exact same age as Savannah was when that whole casino sex-ed story happened.* Kate's first great movie love was *Ghostbusters,* which she watched to the point where Madeline thought she might lose her grip if she heard that tune and that refrain, "who you gonna call," one more time. Then, just as suddenly as Kate's deep allegiance to *Ghostbusters* had emerged, it vanished. Kate switched to *The Little Mermaid.*

Kate did not just watch. She became thoroughly immersed. She had an entire set of costumes and dress-up clothes and pretend furs and pink plastic shoes that she would line up across the floor, and she would stop the movie at each scene change, so she could put on the proper costume. She sang every song and acted out the entire story as well. By the time the mermaid married the prince, Kate was wearing a pink gown with gold stars all over it and a shiny silver crown on her head. She puckered up her lips and leaned her head way out to give her prince a sweet, pretend kiss. Madeline saw all of this as she sat on the couch folding laundry.

When Madeline watched those movies with Kate, she saw them through Kate's eyes. At first, they were brand new, and every single thing was a wonder, a miracle. Then, they became familiar enough to feel like home, but still funny enough to be surprising—every time—and she continued to see things she hadn't seen before. But with more time, and more repetition, the point came when she began to think her brain would ooze out her nose and ears if she had to sit in the presence of those same words for another minute. *Quite a bit like life,* Madeline thought.

When Savannah pushed the button that abruptly ended her call, she said, "That was my dad. I was asking him what I should have for lunch."

"Your dad?"

"Uh-huh."

"Your father?"

"Uh-huh."

"You were asking your father what you should have for lunch."

Savannah could see that it wasn't really a question, so she didn't answer.

"Your father, as in, the guy who put you on an airplane the minute he found out you were pregnant? Who said that you were dead to him? That father?"

"Uh-huh. He wasn't a very big help. MadMad, what do you think I should have for lunch?"

"Oh, no. No, no. I'm not playing that game with you."

Savannah heaved a tremendous sigh, rolled her eyes, and headed for the kitchen. An advertisement came on the television just then. A group of people were seated around a table, completely frozen in time. One of them was caught in the middle of spilling a pitcher of water, the first drop just about to hit. Another person was captured in midair, kicking up his heels, his hair standing straight up in all directions. He was at the highest point, held in the split second before he started down. Yet another person tipped his chair so far back that he was about to tumble over backward; he was caught at the tipping point, held right in the balance. There was one more person. The only one who could move. He was able to walk around this frozen scene, check it from every angle, and ponder what might happen next. He could take all the time in the world to figure it out.

"Oh, my God! MadMad, come in here! Come see what Claire got!" Savannah called from the kitchen.

"This is my favorite! MadMad, look!" Savannah stood back from the refrigerator and held something out in her hand.

"What the heck is that?" Madeline said.

"What is that? *That* is rice pudding! Rice pudding!"

Savannah held a little plastic cup, the kind that Madeline

used to put in John and Kate's lunch boxes, filled with applesauce. Savannah peeled off the silver top and dipped her finger in the lumpy, ivory goo. "Oh, my God, that is good. You gotta try it. Go ahead! Dip your finger!"

"Um, no thanks, I don't really like rice pudding. Never have."

"Ah, are you sure? This stuff is awesome!"

The truth was: Madeline loved rice pudding.

When she and her husband Jeff first moved into the house, and John was a baby, they loved going to a neighborhood diner run by a Greek family that prided itself on its homemade rice pudding. Every time they came through the door, the middle-aged, mustached Greek owner with the sad eyes called out from the far side of the main dining room, "Johhhhhhhhh-hhhhhh-neeeeeeeeeeeeeee" in a booming and festive voice, as if the party could now begin. He snapped his fingers for someone to bring a high chair for John and reached into the pocket of his permanently creased slacks for a balloon. While Madeline and Jeff settled John into the high chair and situated themselves in the booth, the owner blew the balloon into a long thin tube and, with a few deft twists and turns, produced a balloon creature of astonishing complexity—to John's enormous delight. He placed the creation on the tray of John's high chair with a ceremonial flourish and vanished to the nether regions of his domain.

John had been a breeze to take to restaurants because his young appetite was, quite frankly, enormous. He was content to sit and eat for as long as the adults cared to stay, so Madeline and Jeff tackled their Big Food, as they called it, with leisurely relish. There was no question that rice pudding would finish the meal, and a glorious finish it was.

They groaned in satisfaction the entire walk home, doing their best to navigate John's stroller with one hand so they could clasp their own hands fast together.

Savannah said, "Shit girl, you're missing it. I'm telling you, this is the best stuff ever. Last chance before I finish it off."

Savannah again held out the little plastic cup. "Thanks, sweet pea. You finish it. I really don't like rice pudding," Madeline said.

Savannah's smile was hugely content, the crown atop her immense belly. Madeline wobbled, struggled, in a way that was not visible, in order to remain standing. *I wish I wish I wish I could believe this. I wish I could believe that there was some possible happy ending here. That this baby in front of me can somehow take care of her own baby. That there will be balloon-animal, rice-pudding moments in their lives.*

## Chapter 24

*My mother approached the task of preparing three meals a day for growing children with fervor and precision. Everything that was put in front of us, every meal, contained a meticulously constructed, well-rounded, visually pleasing combination of food and drink that also held an appropriate calorie content in a nutritionally perfect amalgam. The chewable vitamins that I was so crazy about were entirely superfluous, I'm sure. I was in such glowing good health and full of bouncy energy as a young child, my grandmother suggested to my mother that perhaps the vitamins were not such a good idea. She was the mean grandmother; my other grandmother tickled my feet all day long, if I wanted, and would never have said such a thing. So it was only when my parents repeatedly questioned the bruises on her legs that she broke down and confessed that my brother was regularly kicking her. Nice grandmother.*

*Not that my mother wasn't a big believer in the Treat—she was. We went to the local bakery every week and always had a well-stocked supply of cookies in the house. We were allowed to have one cookie—but only one—if we finished everything on our plates. I grew up in a time and a household where this was non-negotiable. You ate what was put in front of you, and you ate it all. My mother maintained this policy with a zero-tolerance stance, even though my brother would regularly throw up stuff he genuinely "didn't care for," in the polite-speak used to describe that whole mess.*

*As early as I can remember, my mother said of her painstakingly planned meals that we simply must eat them, because it was good for our Mr. Man. Mr. Man. Once my mother had made clear the extreme importance of Mr. Man, she was pretty vague concerning details. I sort of understood that there was some...thing...inside of me that demanded satisfaction; after that, I was pretty much left to my own imagination.*

*I was very young. I knew that our bodies were warm inside, way warmer than the air around us. I also had some idea that once we chewed up our food and swallowed it, it went somewhere deep down inside of us. It seemed reasonable to me that there must be a fire deep in my belly and that fire needed to be fed on a regular basis or it would go out. (We had a fireplace in my house, and once in a while my parents would let me feed pieces of paper into the dying embers, making a game out of seeing how long I could wait and still get the next piece of paper to ignite. Wait too long, and poof, done, out of luck, fire out.) Well, of course I didn't think there was a nice suburban home fireplace inside my body. I thought it probably looked more like an igloo-shaped pizza oven.*

*I watched a lot of cartoons. I imagined Mr. Man looked pretty much like Wimpy from Popeye—without the suit. I thought he probably wore a plain white T-shirt and work pants. After all, it was hot down there, and he had a ceaseless and essential job to do—you need to be comfortable for that.*

*When I was the same age as Savannah is now—Savannah, who is seven months pregnant, Savannah, whom we are constantly trying to feed—I decided I was getting a little over pudged. I went on a diet. I ate Special K for breakfast, had salad and iced tea for lunch, and ate my mother's home-cooked regular dinner, minus the usual dessert Treat. The pounds flew off of me. But when I had lost the amount of weight I originally wanted to lose, I couldn't break out of the routine. I couldn't get myself to eat anything besides that bowl of Special K for breakfast. Thinking of eating anything besides my usual lunch salad made me feel sick. I remember trying to get myself to eat an apple. I put that apple on the table beside me and stared a hole through it. Couldn't eat it.*

*I went well beyond runway-model thin.*

*I stopped having periods.*

*It was a hot summer, so I was always wearing shorts. My mother kept saying, "Your legs look fantastic. Just fantastic!"*

*My brother worked away from home that summer. When my parents and I got off the boat on the Canadian island where he'd been for three months, he was waiting to meet us. When he saw me, he was speechless. He gave me a giant hug and told me he wasn't saying another word until I ate something. He turned his back on my parents and led me by the hand to the dining room where lunch was being served. Not one word was spoken, and yet my brother made it clear that he thought my parents were completely crazy for letting this happen. And my mother made it equally clear that he was wildly overreacting. After all, my legs were* GORGEOUS.

## Chapter 25

Madeline watched two squirrels chasing one another across the top of the fence in her yard. They knew in their squirrel way that winter was coming. And what would have been playful frolic a month or so ago had turned to ferocious rivalry over the last seeds and acorns that could mean the difference between a thick padding to burn for the long winter or a skimpy layer of fat—and, a squirrel who would be cold, shivering, and desperate long before the frozen world melted away.

Madeline remembered the day when she had been sitting in the same spot, looking out the same window, at the exact moment when a squirrel lost its balance and dropped like a shot from the branch. "Arrogant acrobatic bastard," she said aloud. She would have expected a frantic scrambling of legs and claws and limbs as the squirrel plummeted, but instead the squirrel immediately assumed the spread-eagle position of a skydiver in free fall. And in that same position it landed with an abrupt stop, right on top of the fence, where it lay panting and dazed.

"Oh for God's sake, squirrel bastard, are you really gonna do this? Are you really gonna make me worry about you?"

All afternoon, the squirrel lay atop the fence, spread out, the ends of its limbs dangling. Madeline checked every hour or so. The squirrel seemed to be panting less. She thought maybe that meant he was dying. Jeff would have called this her Disease of Empathy. Her complete inability to do or think about anything other than a living creature that was suffering and being consumed with trying to determine the Right Thing to Do.

Just as the sun sank low enough to cast the juicy, sumptuous golden glow she loved so much, the squirrel stood up on all four legs and walked the length of the fence as if nothing in the world had ever happened. When he reached the end, he scampered down and hopped across the yard and back up the tree.

The whole thing was so utterly bizarre that Madeline wondered for a second if it had really happened. She would have been the only person, among the billions inhabiting the earth, to see it. It was an event that belonged to her and her alone. But really, it was the same with everything. She was the only one who saw from behind her own eyes. Every one of the times she had looked out the windows of this room, every daring squirrel, blowing branch, falling leaf, every play of light and shadow, every every every thing was a vision, a moment of her life that was hers.

"Hey MadMad," Savannah called from the kitchen, "how much pain do you think a baby really feels? Like if I wanted to get him a tattoo, for instance? I mean, they cut off the ends of their penises, right?"

*She said what?* Madeline thought. *She said* WHAT!

It was as if someone had let go of a Madeline balloon and she was flying around the room, completely out of control and deflating fast. Madeline allowed a thought to enter her head that had been previously absent: *Perhaps this whole thing can't work. This. Whole. Thing.*

Madeline picked up her phone and texted Ellie.

M: This is a disaster. A baby having a baby. DISASTER.

E: Uh oh. What's happening?

M: OK, seriously, Savannah just said she's thinking about getting a tattoo for the baby.

E: Wow. There is definitely no emoji that captures my response to that.

M: ☹

E: Hold it. You're not thinking about trying to adopt this baby are you? Tell me you're not thinking that!

M: Why does everyone keep asking me that?!

E: Because we KNOW you!?!

M: No. Never ever. I'm not that good of a person.

E: Just please please keep reminding yourself of that.

M: You're a true friend.

## Chapter 26

"I **don't** know how much more of this I can take
She's filing her nails while they're dragging the lake."

Those two lines from the Elvis Costello song twirled around and around in Madeline's head. Savannah lay on the couch, her belly ridiculous, her teeny feet looking too small to hold even one person upright, let alone one plus. *It's no wonder she has to lie down all the time. Between her goddamn gigantic boobs, her Ripley's-Believe-It-or-Not belly, and her teeny-tiny, itty-bitty midget feet, no wonder she can't stand up. And her razor-cut, rainbow-striped hair and the wad of neon-fucking-blue gum that never fucking leaves her mouth... FUCK YOU. FUCK YOU.* She was not at all sure whom she was addressing in her head—where, exactly, her rage was directed. To nobody. To everybody.

"Savannah," Madeline said in a casual, even tone, "have you thought about...what happens...*after* this baby is born?"

"What do you mean?"

"Well, it just seems like all the focus here is on...getting ready for this kid to be born. Getting all the clothes. The equipment. The *stuff*."

"Yeaaahhhhh?"

"It's like the birth is the big event. The end point." Madeline paused for a response. Savannah cracked her gum. "You know: that's all she wrote; the die is cast; the train has left the station; the little bird has flown; the ship has sailed; the gun is fired; Elvis has left the building."

"MadMad, what are you talking about?"

"I mean, are you thinking about...are you aware, let's say, that there is going to be an actual *baby* that you bring home from the hospital?"

"What do you mean?"

"I mean that there's going to be a baby, a real baby, that you will have to take care of, every day, every night, every minute, all the time."

"I try not to think about that," Savannah said.

"For eighteen years. At least. Three years longer than you've been on this planet so far."

Savannah moved the neon-blue wad from one side of her mouth to the other. "Geez, MadMad I try not to think about that!"

"Yeah, I think that's my point here. I know you're not thinking about it."

"Geez, Mad! What do you want from me? You're making me feel bad!"

An intense pain gathered force on one side of Madeline's head. *My head is gonna explode,* she thought. *It is going to detach from my body and fly apart into a million, icky-gooey-oozy, little pieces. What's the movie where that happens? It's going to splatter against the walls and slap Savannah upside the face.*

"I just think," Madeline said calmly, "that the person I see lying on the couch in front of me doesn't seem like she is ready to have an actual baby. Not one bit ready." Hush rained down into the room like a silent deluge.

## Chapter 27

*Claire* poked at a few dozen cloves of garlic she was roasting in the oven when Madeline came into the kitchen.

"Are you mad at me?" Madeline asked her.

"No," Claire said, in a tone of voice that successfully imparted the following: "I've considered whether I should be mad at you and whether I really am mad at you but am fooling myself into thinking that I'm not and whether I have a lot of very complicated feelings but none of them seems to be anger. So—no."

"Is your sister mad at me?"

Claire poked at the garlic. "You know, Madeline, everyone has told Savannah her whole entire life that she can't do stuff. That she's not good enough."

"I know."

"She's been made to feel like such a piece of shit. From day one. Bounced back and forth."

"I know," said Madeline, feeling like a piece of shit.

"It felt like more-of-the-same to her. Like you're just one

more person who's telling her that she's a total fuckup. That this is yet another thing that she can't do."

Madeline considered for a moment that Claire could easily have said all of those same things about herself. Madeline's anguish did not stem from the withdrawal of her hopeful support of Savannah; the terrible ache rose from the sense of retracting her unwavering support of her daughter-in-law Claire. "But, I'm starting to think maybe she can't do it, Claire. Not because she's a bad human being. Because she's fifteen. Because *no* fifteen-year-old can do this."

"She really, really believes that she can."

"SHE IS FIFTEEN FUCKING YEARS OLD."

"Well I for one am going to do everything I possibly can to help her."

*I am. A. Piece. Of. Shit,* Madeline thought. *But I just can't believe that this will work. Not anymore.*

"And I think we should all be completely committed to that," Claire added. "All of us. To help her as much as we possibly can. Period."

"There isn't enough help, Claire," Madeline said. "Not in the whole world. Not enough to make this work." *How did John do this? How did he manage to find someone who is even more like me than I am? Who really believes that she can stand in the middle of the Niagara River and stop the water from going over the falls through sheer force of will.*

## Chapter 28

From her sometimes bedroom, Savannah could not hear the conversation between Madeline and Claire, but she had a keen sense that they were talking about her.

She minutely examined the tips of her hair for split ends, cracked her gum incessantly and loudly, and thought: *Everybody keeps asking me, all the fucking time they keep asking me, what am I gonna do when the baby's born? What am I gonna do when the baby's born? Fuck should I know what I'm gonna do? Well, I'll tell you what I'm gonna do. Like this is fucking rocket science or something.*

*I'm gonna take care of a baby. That's what I'm gonna do.*

*I hate fucking people sometimes, like all people, like I really mean it, I really do.*

*I'm gonna be a good fucking mother, too. I know I am. A great mother.*

*They're gonna put that baby in my arms, and I'm gonna love him and love him and love him. I'm gonna kiss his little head and play with his toes and rock him and cuddle him and whisper in his little tiny ears. I'm gonna love him up real good. All the time I'm gonna love him up.*

*And he's gonna love me. He's gonna love me like there's no tomorrow, all the time, forever. Because I'm his mommy. I'm his fucking mommy. He'll love me. He'll never leave me. Because he has to. Because I'm his mommy.*

*The future is a giant fucking black hole. Fuck the future. I'm gonna have someone who loves me.*

## Chapter 29

"I ***never*** did this, Maddie, not with any of my four," Billie said. "Maybe you can help her out." And then she added, "I'd sure appreciate it."

Madeline briefly scanned the room. The aunt. The uncle. The cousins. A hospital room, a decent one: big, pastel-y. At least so far as you could tell with the black-out shades drawn and the lights mostly off. Billie darted around, picked up everything in the room, smoothed it out, elaborately folded it, smoothed it out again, then stacked the folded garments into piles, and then re-organized the piles.

Savannah sat cross-legged at the head of the bed, looking even younger and smaller than usual. She stared up at Madeline, expressionless, and motioned Madeline to come closer for a hug. At Savannah's knee, awake in that newborn state of wide-eyed, alert, perfect calm, lay the baby. The Baby. THE BABY.

The brand-new mother's mouth fell slightly open as she looked up at Madeline. Savannah's usual saucer-round, blue eyes were glazed and lost, deep-set within purplish circles of sleep deprivation and the smudged charcoal remains of days-old eyeliner.

"Um, you have to…kind of…give it to him from above. Get it into his mouth from…above." Knowing that her words were meaningless, Madeline made emphatic hand motions of thrusting some imaginary object from a higher to a lower point in the middle of the air of the hospital room, as if this would explain everything. She looked over at Billie. A vein stood out on the side of Billie's neck.

Savannah's mouth opened a hair wider, a combination of determination and bewilderment that stabbed at Madeline's heart.

Savannah lifted her baby and then grabbed her breast and bobbled it at the teeny newborn's head as if it were a water balloon she was hoping to get through the eye of a needle.

"I think your nipple needs to be harder, for him to be able to latch on." Pause. "I think you need to…sort of…pinch your nipple…a little." Madeline made exaggerated pincers of her thumb and fingers.

There was a distinct gap between anything that Madeline said and Savannah's response. It was as if someone hit the pause button for a second—the second it took to penetrate the layers of Vicodin for the pain of her vaginal tear, her exhaustion, her bewilderment, and the effort of trying like hell to soldier through. The pause, during which her face remained entirely blank, was then followed by a perfectly normal reply. Laughter at a funny remark. A nose wrinkle for something gross. After the pause, she was in every way herself. Whether it was the bizarre lag time in Savannah's speech or Billie's perpetual motion or the birth of a baby boy to a fifteen-year-old, an air of taut apprehension pervaded the room. Madeline felt as if she could wave the tension into eddies with her hand.

Savannah made game attempts to adjust the newborn into the crook of her elbow with one arm, while placing her fingers on the outermost edge of her nipple, all the while trying to figure out how to "give it to him from above," like Madeline had said. "Like this?" she asked.

"Um, I'm not sure if he's in a good position. I think his head may be a little bit too far away. From the breast. Your boob."

Savannah looked from her baby boy's head to the breast that lay in her hand to Madeline, and her mouth again fell open. She was exhausted and not understanding and trying so hard and wanting to try even harder and wanting to give up.

Madeline looked around the room and said to Savannah, "Would it help...do you want me to get on the bed with you?"

"Yeah, yeah, yeah, yeah," she said. "Yes."

"Yeah, you go head, Mad." Billie waved Madeline toward the bed, her fists clenching and re-clenching as she spoke.

The aunt, the uncle, and the cousins, who had been murmuring among themselves with downcast eyes, decided at this point they would excuse themselves and get refreshments. Madeline edged over to the side of the bed and sat down with a tender tentativeness. Seated a respectful distance from Savannah, Madeline tucked one leg underneath the other, letting her foot dangle casually off the side, in an attempt to project calm confidence. And with the simple movement of raising her rear end slightly off the bed to tuck her leg, she got her first real glimpse of newborn Dylan Roy.

Tears threatened to well, pour, spring from her eyes. The sum of tears inside her threatened to flood the room. Billie still holding a pile of meticulously folded *things,* Savannah still cross-legged on the bed with her mouth agape—they would be swept up in a great salty tide and whisked down the corridor, past roomfuls of astonished new mothers cradling infants, while Madeline swooped up Dylan and saved him.

She saves him. She seizes him and holds him and swaddles his blanket tight and rubs her cheek against his newborn hair and smells his skin and makes a pact, a pact that very instant that she will do anything in the world to protect him, anything at all, forever, she will do anything she needs to do for the rest of time as long as there is time, because he is there and he is perfect and he is new and everything is possible for him. Everything. He will have a good life, he will—

"MadMad? What should I do?"

Madeline fixed her gaze intently on Dylan, as if pondering the question quite seriously, until the dam inside of her that threatened to burst proved it could hold.

"Um, let's try again."

Savannah went through each step—positioning Dylan, squeezing her nipple, then maneuvering the outer third of her breast so it came down to Dylan's mouth from above. After each separate move, she looked back to Madeline, and Madeline nodded.

Savannah squeezed her nipple and urged it toward Dylan's mouth. Dylan instinctively nuzzled against it, rooting, moving his head from side to side, each time latching on for a mere second, only to have it slip from his lips.

"I don't know what I'm doing wrong," Savannah said.

"You're both getting it. Really. You both just need practice. And time," Madeline said.

"Can you help me?"

"Help you?" Madeline said. "Like, how?"

"I don't know. Can you...show me?" Holding her breast in one hand and the infant in the other, Savannah gestured with her head.

Madeline shifted on the bed so she sat close against Savannah, whose nipple had softened and flattened once again. "Ok you need to squeeze your nipple again. So it's hard. Again."

"Can you do it?"

"You want me to do it?" Madeline attempted to say casually.

Savannah nodded. "Yeah. Can you just...do the whole thing?"

"Do the whole thing?"

Madeline put a great deal of work, an enormous effort, into acting as if this were the most natural thing in the world, as if she had done this a million times. Madeline reached for the breast of a fifteen-year-old girl. She squeezed the nipple, and she directed the breast from a position slightly above Dylan's head into his eager, expectant mouth. For a few fleeting seconds, Madeline felt she had been given a magnificent gift. In a featureless hospital room, with an exhausted adolescent mother whose breast she held in her own hand, she had been granted a moment of profound grace.

"It's starting to hurt," Savannah said.

"Yeah. Well. Sure. It's all new. It can hurt a little for a while," Madeline recognized the voice she had used so many times with her own two children, when they were their most scared, their most in need of comforting encouragement—most in need of a mother.

"No, I mean, it *really* hurts," Savannah said.

"Oh. Are you doing OK?"

"They gave me this cream to put on. In case it hurt," Savannah said.

"Oh. Great."

"I think I should put it on now."

"Oh. You want to stop now?" Madeline asked "Sure. That's fine. That's totally fine. Everybody thinks it's gonna be totally natural, like it's instinct or something. It takes a while. I mean, you're both doing this for the first time! It...takes a while."

"I want to try this cream. Can you take him and try to burp him?" Savannah asked. "I'm going in the bathroom."

"You're asking me if I'll hold him?"

Billie turned her back and marched to the far corner of the room. Savannah eased herself off the bed with her hands and said, "Hey, MadMad, can you do me a favor? Can you ask them if I can have some more painkillers? Everything's hurting."

"Sure. Of course." Madeline cradled Dylan in the crook of her arm, madly in love.

## Chapter 30

*You* could see it right away when Dylan was born. There was something strange with one side of his face. Even as a brand-new, tiny little newborn, barely out of Savannah's body long enough to have gotten cleaned up and dried off and experienced the feeling of air in his own lungs. Wriggling around, even though he was straight-jacket-swaddled inside the hospital blankets, you could see there was something going on. When Dylan Roy began to cry, yawn, or let out a holler, one side of his mouth did not cooperate with the other side. The uncooperative side stayed perfectly, utterly still. The other side did every bit of the work.

The nurses who came into Savannah's room seemed to have their eyebrows permanently raised. They looked mostly at the floor but stole the most furtive of glances at each other as they passed. The doctors were in and out in a flash, all efficiency and practiced professionalism. If anybody noticed that one side of the baby's mouth was refusing to join forces with the other, no one said a word. None of the visitors paid any attention to Dylan's face as they paraded in and out of Savannah's hospital room to examine or coo at the baby, not when he was going home with a mother who had barely reached fifteen years of age

As Dylan grew, he did all of the things that babies do right on time, as if he was reading directly from a handbook. He smiled and gurgled and cooed from his earliest days. It seemed that he was going to have a great deal to say when he grew, as he practiced and tested out different sounds he could make nearly all of the time.

When anyone looked at the left side of Dylan's face as he chortled away, they could see the full rainbow of life's feelings passing through his sparkling eyes and across his laugh-pinched cheeks and on his lively, little mouth. But if they focused on the other side, they would have seen that the right half of his face remained stone still. One eyelid blinked just a hair slower than the other, one cheek lay flat, and half of his mouth stayed as limp and unmoving as a fish too long out of the water.

Dylan had been born with a couple of facial nerves that weren't connected the way they were supposed to be.

*It seems like Dylan himself is split; half of him seems thrilled to have been given this life and the other half doesn't seem so damn sure,* Madeline thought. *Or, maybe there is a God after all, and maybe He has a weird-ass sense of humor. Or maybe He's just an Old-Testament, malicious motherfucker.*

# Chapter 31

Claire camped out at the hospital with Savannah and newborn Dylan around the clock; so Madeline and Dan had the house to themselves for several days. The two of them sat at the dining room table one evening, blowing on their spoonfuls of piping hot, warmed-up lentils. The same lentil dish Dan had cooked for her and served her by candlelight shortly after they met. The same lentil dish Dan had cooked at least once a week, every week, since.

"So, have you thought about when you're going to tell your ex that you're in a new quote, unquote relationship? Like you mentioned last night?" Madeline asked.

Dan's spoon stopped in midair. He leaned all the way back in his chair. "Why in the world would I tell her that?" He looked at Madeline as if she were utterly mad.

It was Madeline's turn to sit back in her chair. She scanned Dan's face for some flicker that he was pulling her leg, a flicker that was not there. "You said you had been thinking about it. You said you thought you needed to tell her. *Yesterday,* you said it."

"I couldn't possibly have said that, because there is no possible way that I would think of telling her." Dan's delivery manifest bewilderment, but also an unmistakable tinge of rage. It was the end of any further conversation during that evening's lentil dinner.

Madeline's thoughts roiled. She certainly knew by then that Dan had a seriously crappy memory, but this went well beyond the usual. It had been *one night* before, as they had sat in those same chairs at that same dining room table, digging into take-out food from their favorite local Chinese spot. Through a mouthful of Szechuan broccoli, Dan had said, "I've been thinking about Nancy. I've been thinking that I need to tell her about you. I mean, even though the relationship has been over for years, her friendship is really important to me. I think it's the right thing to do. I need to tell her."

Madeline had said something along the lines of "oh" the previous evening, not actually caring one way or another if Dan told some ex-lover across the pond about their...whatever-it-was. Perhaps this would have mattered to her a great deal if times were a bit different, she reflected. But once you've had police officers threatening to lock you up, and child protective services filling out forms while sitting at that same dining room table, and a teeny-footed baby taking care of her own baby—once your life has become a surreal intermingling of prosaic joys juxtaposed with the continual sense of a ticking time bomb—well, priorities tend to shift.

*What the fuck is happening here?* Madeline wondered. *He*

*seriously can't remember what he said last night? Is this guy completely losing it?* A momentary fear had gripped her that she might not even be safe with him. But just as quickly, a different and grimmer picture entered her mind. What if her memory was just as lousy as Dan's? What if she just happened to remember that particular conversation, whereas there were countless others that she did not recall? What if, God forbid, she and Dan actually had the same conversations over and over and over? And, if that wasn't already the case, was that the inevitable future?

Madeline remembered an anthropology course she had taken many years before in college, titled Varying Meanings of Life and Death. She pictured herself sitting in her college bedroom chair—the chair that her parents had let her take from her bedroom at home—reading the textbook. The super-comfy armchair with the flesh-colored, bizarre nautical-patterned slipcover. She had run her fingers along the welted seams of that chair while she read her way through four years of books. She saw herself in her beloved chair, in her Spartan room, holding the textbook with its bright red cover. She had ended up fascinated with the class, pouring over the descriptions of other lands and other people and regaling her roommates at dinner with tidbits she could not wait to share.

The particular idea that bubbled up from deep memory while she pondered Dan's mystifying memory lapse was this: there was a society in Spain—she was fairly sure it was Spain—where the people believed that life and death are not moments, but rather processes that occur over many years. A "person" emerges gradually during childhood as life grows; likewise, life retreats from a person bit by bit as he or she ages.

*When does life begin to retreat?* Madeline wondered. *Has this started already?*

## Chapter 32

As Madeline double-checked the cantankerous coffeepot before hitting the start button, she felt pretty certain that she heard a susurration coming from the back room. That's the word that came into her head—susurration. *Is that another leap from deep, long-term memory of vocabulary study, or is that one of the weird things Jeff used to say? No,* she thought, *what Jeff said was tintinnabulation. "The tintinnabulation of the bells, bells, bells."*

Poking her head around the corner from the kitchen, Madeline discovered Savannah curled into a tight little ball on the couch with baby Dylan swaddled into a tight little ball and sleeping in the curve of Savannah's belly.

Savannah opened her eyes. "Ugh. I didn't sleep at all last night."

"You just never know who you're gonna wake up to find in this house these days," Madeline said. "How come you're not in the bedroom?"

"I love this couch."

"Well, that has pretty much always seemed to be the case. Hey, how did you get here, anyway?"

"I took the bus. A bunch of different buses, actually," Savannah said.

Madeline considered the distance from Billie's house to her own—and the complexity of managing this distance with a newborn, in the winter, in the nighttime—for a moment before she asked, "Do you want some coffee?"

"I'm gonna try to fall back asleep. As long as Dylan's still sleeping. But I will want some, later, for sure. With a ton of milk and sugar."

"Are you actually gonna drink it?" Madeline asked. "It seems like it's kind of a family tradition for you and your sister to *not* drink your coffee. Judging by what I toss down the sink."

"No, I'm gonna need it. I'll drink it. Promise."

"OK, I'll let you get back to sleep," Madeline said as she returned to the kitchen.

A little voice, the voice of a child, said, "MadMad, I think we may be here for a while. Me and Dylan."

"What do you mean?" Madeline asked.

"Meaning, like, for good."

Madeline started to ask Savannah what had happened, but she stopped herself. *What does it really matter? It was bound to come to this. Always, since the beginning of the beginning, it was bound to come to this.* In one sense, Madeline believed it would be easier to keep an eye on things with Savannah under her roof. In another sense, she thought: *Welcome to the beginning of the train wreck.*

"Your sister says she's here 'for good' now. Those were her exact words." Madeline met Claire at the door to say this; she did not even wait until Claire had kicked off her boots or had a second to shake off the early winter chill.

"Yeah. I know," Claire said. "She texted me."

"Claire, what does this mean?"

"In what sense?" Claire asked.

"In what sense! Well, skipping for a minute what the hell might've happened—because I'm not so sure I want to know—last I heard, I was harboring a fugitive runaway and was gonna get tossed in the slammer any minute if Savannah even considered calling this place home."

"Yeah, I recall," said Claire.

"Claire, seriously, I can't handle the police coming here. Or child services. I mean it. I can't have that happen. Again."

"I know." Claire met Madeline's eyes for the first time. "I really don't think it will."

"Well, how can that be true? What could possibly have changed?"

"What's changed," Claire said, "is that it seems the Department of Children and Family Services has assessed the 'situation' and decided to look the other way."

"What the hell does that mean?" Madeline bit at her lip.

"It means they seem to have figured out a few things about the whole situation, meaning my mother—enough to just sort of ignore the fact that Savannah might not actually be living with her," Claire said.

"OK, but what if Billie calls the cops? Reports her as a runaway? Billie's still her mother and legal guardian. The cops would have to step in. Savannah's still fifteen and still not allowed to live on her own, baby or no baby."

"I'm pretty sure the cops have been made fully aware of the situation, too," Claire said.

"You're shitting me," Madeline said.

"Nope."

"So a couple of months ago, we were all hardened criminals, and now it's OK for a fifteen-year-old kid to be on her own, raising another kid."

"This is all unofficial and off-the-record, of course," Claire replied. "But, yeah, that pretty much sums it up," Claire said.

"Is this good news, Claire?" Madeline asked. "I mean, really, is any of this good news?"

## Chapter 33

"*MadMad,* can you take him, please? Can you come up here and get him?" Savannah called through the closed door of her bedroom. Her groggy voice wafted down the stairway and through the kitchen, finding Madeline savoring her morning coffee at the sunroom table.

Upstairs Madeline opened the door to find Savannah already holding Dylan in outstretched arms. And—surprise!—a young man, a boy really, lying face down and splayed across the mattress in his underwear. "I didn't get any sleep at all last night. Is it OK for you to take him for a while? Do you have to go to work soon?"

"No, it's fine," Madeline said. "It's...really fine."

Savannah had already plopped back on the bed and closed her eyes when she mumbled, "There's not a whole lot of formula left."

Madeline grabbed her phone and immediately called Claire at work. "Are you aware that your sister has a gentleman caller who happens to be sharing a bed with her right now? In my house?"

Claire howled, "What? OMG, it must be Jaime!"

"Who the fuck is Jaime?"

"Do you remember that kid she met in the park when she was here a couple of summers ago?" Claire asked. "That's Jaime. She ran into him again. Same park."

Madeline groaned. "Terrific. I'm not sure that really explains why they're in bed together. With Dylan. Except without Dylan now. I have him."

"Do you mind taking care of him?"

"Of course not. But hold on. I thought you guys told me that she had gotten back together with the baby daddy. Which I never understood in the first place since he's two thousand miles away in Arizona."

Claire's shrug was almost audible. "They broke up again. She's pissed at him. I guess she caught him flirting with someone else."

Madeline's retort was more statement than question, "Caught him from two thousand miles away."

"That's probably why she's hanging out with Jaime. 'Cause she's pissed at baby daddy."

"Hanging out in *a bed*."

Again the shrug was nearly audible. "I'll talk to her. I gotta go."

Madeline's own words rang in her head. From a conversation she'd had with Ellie when the inevitable happened. When it became clear that Savannah and Dylan needed to move into the house.

"I can't be a mother to her, Ellie. I won't do that. I'll give them a place to stay and I'll help out with Dylan however and whenever I can cause I'm totally, madly in love with him and because he deserves the absolute best beginning in his little life that all of us can possibly give him, but I'm not gonna be her mother. Not in any way. Claire's gonna have to set the rules and whatever else. I'm not getting into any of that with Savannah."

Madeline wedged her index finger into Dylan's tiny fist so his fingers would curl around it and grip. With her other hand she stroked his cheek, causing him to smile with the half of his mouth that could smile. His eyes fluttered as he attempted to fight off sleep. She treasured these moments when she had the baby to herself, when she could lose herself in her fascination with his every minuscule movement, every slight change of expression that passed across his face. It did not happen often, but now and again at these precious times, it was almost as if the specter of her ex-husband, Jeff, joined her. He sat beside her on the couch, and they gazed down together, lost in the miracle of the tiny life before them.

In the "real" world, the very much flesh-and-blood Dan came into the sunroom and sat on the side not taken up by Jeff's memory ghost. He grasped Dylan's other hand, so they formed a makeshift human chain—three closely bound people who bore no blood relationship to one another. Whether in response to the complexities encircling him, or strictly the result of his own inner rumblings, Dylan wrinkled his face and let out a parade of fussy snorts. Madeline put him on her shoulder and nuzzled her face against his own. "He may be hungry," she said. "I don't have any idea when he had his last feeding." She rolled her eyes. "I mean, some guy named Jaime is upstairs in bed with Savannah."

"WHAT?" Dan blurted.

"Yeah. He's a friend from a couple of summers ago. I guess she ran into him again when she was hanging out in the park. With the baby."

"You've gotta be kidding me. Does Claire know?"

"Yep," Madeline said. "I called her at work. Claire said she'd talk to her and take care of it. Meanwhile...I better make a bottle."

"I'll do it," Dan said.

"Really?" Madeline said. She did delight in this man who had never been around a baby, never held a baby in his entire fifty-five-year-old life. She had observed how he stood at a terrified, awkward distance when he came to the hospital after Dylan was born. She had watched him thaw, gradually at first. She had seen him become mesmerized. She had heard him say, more than once, that maybe, no definitely, if he had met Madeline earlier in his life, the two of them would have made a family together. And here he was, offering to mix a bottle of infant formula for a baby whose fifteen-year-old mother was catching up on her sleep with some lost boy named Jaime, because she was pissed at her baby daddy who had flirted with another girl thousands of miles away.

Dan left the room and returned a few brief seconds later with the empty formula container. "There's no formula left.

None." He displayed the empty container, shaking it around for emphasis.

Madeline sighed heavily.

"She needs to figure this out," Dan said. "She insists she wants this baby, and she needs to figure this out."

"She's fifteen years old," Madeline said. "She ain't gonna figure out shit."

"Well, as long as she's here, she's gonna try." Dan turned on his heels and sprinted up the stairs to the second floor. Madeline held her breath, picturing Dan clenching and unclenching his jaw. The lightness of his knock on Savannah's door surprised Madeline, as did the gentle voice that matched it.

"Savannah?" Dan said. "You need to get up. We're completely out of formula. You need to go get some."

After a short pause, Savannah's groggy voice replied, "OK. I'm up. OK."

Dan remained at her door until he heard a general stirring of activity and then said, "Try to hurry up. Dylan's already hungry."

Dan rejoined Madeline in the sunroom, where Dylan had drifted into a light snooze on her shoulder. "Nicely done," she said. "You handled that really well."

"I think we would have made good parents," Dan said.

"To a fifteen-year-old unwed mother? Great."

"No. You know that's not what I meant. You make all of this look so appealing, Madeline. Like no other choices or other kinds of lives make sense to even consider," he said.

A highly disheveled Savannah appeared in the doorway,

joined at the hip to a skinny wraith of a boy who appeared shrunken and withered, even though he towered over Savannah by ten inches or more.

"I guess we'll have to walk over to the Walgreen's to get some," Savannah said.

"OK. He's fallen asleep. He's fine for now," Madeline said.

"I mean, Claire usually takes me to that place where I can get the formula for free, but there's no way to get there 'cause she's at work, right?" Savannah offered.

"Right," said Dan, before Madeline could answer.

"So I guess we'll walk over to the Walgreen's."

"OK."

"So…I need to borrow the money for it," Savannah said.

"You need to borrow the money?" Madeline asked.

"Don't worry, Claire will pay you back as soon as she gets home. It's usually, like, twenty-five dollars for a container. Can you believe it's so expensive? God, I'm *so* glad we get it free," Savannah said.

"I'm not worried," Madeline said. "Let me rephrase. I'm not worried about getting paid back by Claire."

Dan reached into his pants pocket. "I've got a twenty right here. Do you have the rest, Savannah? Five bucks or so?"

"Um, no, well, I can count up my change," Savannah said. "I might have it."

"Never mind counting change. You can get the rest out of my wallet," Madeline said.

"OK, thanks," Savannah said. "Hey MadMad, can I borrow your jacket? Again?" She giggled.

"So I guess you want us to watch Dylan while you two go off to the store," Dan said.

"Oh. Right. No, we can take him." Savannah glanced at the silent, sunken waif at her side.

"Except I think he barfed all over the carrier. I think I need to wash it."

"No reason to wake a hungry baby to take him outside in a barf-covered carrier. If you guys hurry, I'll have enough time to get to work," Madeline said. "So hurry."

After a general commotion and Savannah making approximately ten times the number of movements as the Wraith, the front door closed behind them. Dylan moved his head and frowned slightly in his sleep.

"Talkative chap, isn't he?" Dan said.

"Jaime? Yeah. He's grown about a foot and is otherwise unrecognizable from the kid I met a couple of years ago, but I don't remember him saying a single word back then either. He just sort of followed Savannah from room to room. She ate it up at first, but then she got more and more annoyed and ended up treating him pretty much like shit—calling and texting other guys the whole time he was around—until he vanished. It was an interesting relationship."

"Ah. Well, it makes sense then that they've hooked up again," Dan said.

The two of them chuckled softly. "It's kind of not funny," Madeline said.

"It's not funny at all," Dan said. "That's why we're laughing."

Later that evening, when Claire was back from her double

shift at work, she waited until Savannah had taken Dylan upstairs for the night, and Dan had wandered off to visit his brother, before she said to Madeline, "I talked to her. You don't need to worry. You won't be seeing Jaime spending any more nights here. She's very clear on that."

"Great," Madeline said.

"She's not sleeping with him, by the way," Claire said. "I talked to her about it. They're not sleeping together."

"Well, technically, they are. Sleeping together," Madeline countered.

"You know what I mean," Claire said.

"I do know what you mean. I guess I'm a wee bit surprised that you believe that. I mean, I'm not doubting for a second that she told you that, but we're talking about a kid who got pregnant before she blew out fifteen candles on her cake."

"I do believe her. I really think they're just friends. Turns out he has a baby, too. A daughter who's around a year old. He's not with the baby mama anymore. But I guess he sees her pretty often."

"Oh, lovely. Heartwarming. So they're bonding over being incredibly, inappropriately young and clueless teenage single parents."

"She really needs to make friends here. She's gotta have some people her own age to hang out with, start building a life for herself here. She can't just hang out with the baby and with us all the time. I think this is a really good thing," Claire said.

"I'm sorry. Do I sound sarcastic and bitter? Perhaps it's because...I'm sarcastic and bitter," Madeline said.

"I told Savannah that he can't be sleeping over again," Claire said.

"Thank you. Yeah, I was not, in fact, prepared for the sight of a scrawny youngster in his boxer shorts when she called me to come and get Dylan." Madeline added, "At least he was face down."

"Ouch," Claire said. "Besides, the doctors and nurses told her over and over again that she can't have any sexual contact at all whatsoever for at least six weeks, until she's had her checkup. Then I'm going with her, and I'll make sure they put her on birth control. Believe me, I'll make sure. The last thing she wants right now is another baby."

"I hope you're right," Madeline said. Claire's unrelenting faith in her sister was truly a force of nature. "You still really believe that this can work out, don't you?"

"Of course I do," said Claire. "She's gonna need a lot of help and support, don't get me wrong, of course I know that. But we'll find parenting classes for her and get her hooked up with other young moms and get her working on her GED. We just need to believe in her—all of us—and we need to let her know that we believe in her. And we need to pitch in. However we can."

Madeline scanned Claire's face, her pit-bull determination and her massive heart written all over it. "Claire," Madeline said with the gentleness of a lullaby, "I think there is something that you don't understand. I think you just don't get that Savannah is not *you.* She just isn't. You have so much...grit... more than pretty much anybody I've ever known, and you keep thinking that Savannah does, too. But she doesn't. *Maybe* you could have had a baby when you were as young as she is and actually made a good life for both of you—maybe—but she can't. She just...can't."

"I know she's not me. But that doesn't mean she can't do this."

Madeline and Claire looked up to see Savannah rounding the corner, holding a wide-awake Dylan and laughing. "He is so fun," she said. "I don't think I want to have my kids be really far apart, you know? I think it would be great to have them kind of close together."

## *Chapter 34*

By the second week of December, Madeline felt as if she had fast-forwarded through a ten-year marriage in just slightly more than three months, with its compendium of petty annoyances, a rising tide of deeper resentments, the comfort of shared history, and continually fluctuating warmth.

Once it had become too cold to swim in the lake, Dan spent long, lazy days in the kitchen, carrying on animated conversations with himself while he fussed over his lentils. Madeline recalled how immensely charmed she had been when Dan took over her kitchen for an entire afternoon the first time he cooked the dish for her in September; by mid-December the noisy stream of words made her seriously question his sanity as well as provoking the hairs on the back of her neck to stand at attention.

The ticket had been purchased—the ticket for the airplane that would whisk Dan from Chicago to a tropical paradise for the brutal winter that lay ahead. January 4, he would be gone, poof. Madeline teetered precariously on the brink of wondering how she could possibly tolerate three more weeks of his off-key humming, his utter failure to get her jokes, his flossing ritual. When he shuffled off to the bathroom each night to brush and floss for an absurd amount of time, it set her own teeth on edge to such a degree she felt certain her back molars would shatter into bits.

In the evenings, the two of them would sit on the sofa. Savannah and the baby dozed together in John's old bed upstairs. Claire worked one of her two jobs—or ran hither and yon trying her best to manage her own and several others' lives. Dan invariably began his kneading of Madeline's thigh, or his massaging of each individual finger—a perpetual motion machine of continual buzzy movement. The sadistic mosquito that senses when you are just about to drift off to sleep and then whispers in your ear. *For crying out loud,* Madeline thought to herself, *no wonder this guy meditates. This is a man who hasn't known one moment of stillness in his entire life.*

She set her jaw against his very existence, calculating how she would bear the number of minutes until she could suggest that they call it a day, go upstairs for the night. At least the flossing ritual would offer her some peace. And then, the solace of a lonely sleep with Dan's inhumanly perfect profile on the pillow beside her.

Madeline sighed. She rested her hand on Dan's thigh for a second—a friendly gesture—and told him she was heading upstairs. "Be right up," Dan said, without turning his head from the TV. "I want to catch a bit more of this, if you don't mind."

Madeline was out of the room when she said, over her shoulder, "I don't mind a bit."

When Dan entered the bedroom, Madeline was idly leafing through a magazine. In a different mood, she would have endorsed this particular journalistic effort as a guilty pleasure, a concept and a reality she wholeheartedly supported. Tonight, leaning against the tower of pillows on her bed, she despised its banality, its endlessly recycled topics meant to appeal to the dark recesses of shame and anxiety amalgamated into the creature known as the American Woman. Which meant, of course, she hated herself for reading it. For falling prey to its sunny, adjective-laden, exclamation-point-heavy!!!, **bold** and *Stylized-Font-Loaded* BULLSHIT about how to eat, dress, exercise, cut, coif, bleach, dye, tweeze, think, and talk as one's best possible self, including, needless to say, fucking like a goddess.

"Are you in for the night?" Dan asked her.

"Yup." She pretended intense concentration on her hated rag.

Dan switched off the light and began to undress. He undid his pants, which were baggy enough that they dropped immediately to the floor. Madeline unconsciously looked up at the sound of the belt's thunk against the wood. She was confronted with the silhouette of his body, naked now from the waist down. Somehow the fact that Dan did not wear underwear—ever—gave her a thrill that pierced clear through the layers of annoyance. It felt like an exquisite finger had touched a spot deep inside her belly. *God-fucking-damn it,* she thought, *this guy still does it for me.*

Dan crossed his arms and grabbed the sides of his shirt and pulled it over his head, rocking his hips first forward—just slightly—and back again along with the movement of the shirt as it climbed his abdomen, his chest, and down his arms to the reaches of his fingertips. He gathered his clothes from the floor and stood in the dim light of the room with such an utter lack of self-consciousness or guile that the ridiculous word "swoon" actually flashed across Madeline's mind.

As if pulled by some string attached to that inner finger, Madeline's foot inched up her other leg to the knee and fell to the side, leaving her legs open, wide, facing toward Dan.

Sometimes it is a smell or the particular angle of the sun's light or the sound of a door closing—some thing that makes its way through the store of life's memories and touches something deep, far, previously lost. In this case, it was the movement, the precise position of her legs.

The memory was from years before. Her still-husband Jeff had come—had made an appointment to come—to the house while the children were at school, in order to gather some of his things. She had not known exactly what to do with herself and had gone into the bedroom to escape, to stay out of the way of this stranger she had been married to for more than twenty years.

He came into the bedroom. He asked some question or other.

She had no idea exactly what stirred her. The slight stoop of his shoulders she had not noticed before. The fact that he wore his glasses all the time these days. The awkward boyish uncertainty that made him speak just a bit too loud. The words were out of her mouth without her own knowledge, it seemed.

"Jeff, let's make love." And for some reason she added, "Please."

Her leg had moved up, her knees had fallen open, into that exact position as the words escaped her mouth.

Jeff sighed. "I can't." He shook his head and looked at the floor. "I just can't."

"Twenty-one years, Jeff. Twenty. One. Years. I have no idea, no memory, of the last time we made love. It seems like this is something I should have. We should have."

He sighed again, shook his head, and suddenly looked much smaller, much older.

"You mean because of her," Madeline said.

Jeff said nothing.

"That's what you mean, isn't it? You mean because of her you will not make love with me. With your wife."

"I don't want you to think for a second that our marriage unraveled because of her. I can't have you think that," Jeff said.

"That's an interesting choice of words—you can't have me think that."

"Madeline, for God's sake."

"It doesn't seem like an unreasonable thing to ask. To know it will be the last time. To have a memory of it." She added, "We are still married, you know. Meaning that you're already a cheater. Meaning that if you're trying to avoid thinking of yourself as a cheater, well, too late."

Jeff walked out of the room and left the house.

Madeline remained on the bed, in the position with her legs open, for a long time.

No.

That's not what happened.

That was what a large part of Madeline had wanted to happen. Part of her still wanted to believe that the man she had spent the past twenty-some years with was an honorable man, a man who had strayed into a new love and who had declared his undying loyalty to that love, in the same way that he once had declared it to her.

The truth was this. The minute her knee dropped and her legs parted, she called out her still-husband's name, "Jeff," just as he came in to ask a question. He took one step closer to the bed. And then he took another.

She remembered the tentativeness of their first touches. The awkward reaching of their tongues, venturing for the first time in a long while inside the surface of one another. Her head awhirl in a cacophony of recalled experience, a blur of lightning-quick images. The two of them making love. Fucking. Doing both at once.

"Dan," she said, "come here."

She ran her fingers lightly along the underside of his penis from the base to the tip and back.

He leaned his head back and said, "Ah, Madeline. Your touch."

No.

That's not what happened.

She and Jeff did not make love. She would never know, would have no memory, of the last time. A tear ran down her cheek onto the pillow. She wiped it away to the sound of Dan's gentle snore.

## Chapter 35

*Madeline* thought she heard footsteps running up and down the stairs as she folded the clothes in the basement laundry room.

Madeline remained a tenacious believer in the power of simple pleasures. Folding fresh, clean clothes into an architecturally arranged, enormous pile that she could carry in one trip, sniffing deep into the fragrant laundry, always tickled her. She had to rest her chin on the top of the heap and bear down in order to manage the load. Her arms carefully cradled the bottom of the stack. She planted her chin and began her ascent of the first of two flights of stairs between the laundry room and its final destination in her bedroom.

Rounding the landing on the second flight of stairs, thinking to herself, *Ha, nearly there and not a single sock teetering,* Madeline caught a glimpse of the wild turkey feather on the sofa, where Savannah had been running it back and forth across Dylan's cheeks while she wrinkled up her nose and cooed at him.

The turkey feather. The souvenir from the day she and Dan drove to the Lake Michigan dunes and took that magnificent hike.

There were times when Madeline exhibited an inappropriately optimistic view of things past, which ranged from sweetly touching to downright frightening. For instance, there was the now-infamous time when John read *Of Mice and Men* for his eighth-grade English class. From an early age, John had possessed an uncanny ability to predict the outcome of a story from very near the beginning of a book, movie, TV show, etc. He would pause the movie, or put down the book, and would not go any further until he asked if the outcome was going to be what he expected. And he then considered whether he wanted to go forward and face the inevitable, or whether he chose to take a pass. He asked Madeline if *Of Mice and Men* was going to have the tragic, heartbreaking ending he foresaw. And Madeline, over the course of the many years since she had read it, had somehow spun the story into a sparse, entirely lovely Steinbeck tale about the love and devotion of two brothers. Epic fail. Even as a nearly six-feet-tall fourteen-year-old who shaved, John took to his bed immediately after dinner the night he finished the book.

Another time Madeline had gotten serious about her responsibility to ensure that her growing children experienced the wide range of world cinema, and not simply the mainstream American extravaganzas that they loved. Where to start, she had wondered. Something with a simple story, little dialogue, stunning visuals, and the far slower, more languid pace that characterized films from nearly every other country. *I've got it,* she thought, remembering a film she had seen in college, Nicholas Roeg's *Walkabout.* Somehow, in her memory, the movie had metamorphosed into a visually lovely, mystical trek through the Outback where two lost children follow a young Aboriginal boy back to home and safety. She would never forget John's and Kate's expressions when they turned to her, five minutes into the film, their mouths open, their faces pale and questioning. Madeline's rosy memory had completely erased the part where the father drives the children into the Outback, kicks them out of the car, attempts to shoot them, and then proceeds to douse the car with gasoline and set it ablaze before shooting himself. While his children watch.

So there was much precedent for Madeline remembering, at least at first, a happy scene when Savannah tickled Dylan's newborn cheeks with the turkey feather while cooing and giggling at her baby boy. But as Madeline negotiated the final half flight of stairs, she remembered the actual scenario between Savannah and her and the turkey feather.

"He's wonderful, Savannah. Completely wonderful," Madeline had said. Dylan followed the sound of Madeline's voice with his eyes and smiled.

"Yeah...," Savannah said.

"What's wrong? You sound like something's wrong."

"Nah. I was just remembering when my dad used to tickle me...."

"Oh. Are you…missing him?" Madeline wasn't sure how to read Savannah's seeming wistfulness, let alone what in the world to say.

"Ha! Miss him? Nah. I mean, he was an OK dad, I guess. Sometimes."

"Was he, Savannah?"

"I mean, yeah. No. I don't know. Things got pretty bad there, sometimes." Savannah stopped stroking Dylan with the feather and laid it beside her on the sofa. She wrapped her hands around Dylan's arms and held fast. "You know he called the cops on me, right?"

"Yeah, I heard that," Madeline said.

"You know they took me away? Put me into juvey? You know, juvenile detention?"

"No," Madeline replied. "I didn't know that."

"Yep," Savannah said. " 'Cause I was late coming home. He told the cops I was all violent and out of control. Ha! *He's* the one who's out of control. After a few days, the cops told me I had my choice, I could go home or I could stay there. Guess what? I stayed. For, like, more than a week."

"Really?"

"I knew better than to go home, until he, you know, cooled off." Savannah shrugged. "I knew he'd just…be all physical with me."

"What do you mean?"

"He'd…you know…shove me around…a little"

"Shove you around? What are we talking about here?" Madeline asked.

"I never had to go to the hospital or anything like that...," Savannah said. "Well, just that one time."

"Are you serious?" Madeline said, loud enough to startle Dylan. "What happened?"

"I got taken away. But they sent me back."

Madeline's head spun. "How badly did you get hurt?"

"Oh. Nothing broken. Well, just a hairline fracture, they said. Plus stitches and stuff."

Madeline did not know what to say. Inside her head, she said, *When did my whole fucking life turn into the fucking Jerry Springer show?* But the words that actually emerged from her mouth were: "I'm so sorry you had to go through stuff like that, Savannah," which seemed woefully, tragically inadequate, but she said them nonetheless. Madeline added, "With both of your parents."

"Yeah. Whatever." Savannah shrugged again. "Now I got this little guy," she said, as if that explained, as well as solved, every single thing.

Madeline cajoled the laundry down the short hall and into the bedroom, where she immediately noticed...some lack. Something not there that had been there before, the empty space shouting at her. It took her a moment to realize what was absent—Dan's various paper bags, there in the corner since he had unexpectedly taken up residence a couple of months earlier.

Before Madeline had time to ponder, she saw a single white page, its ragged edge clearly ripped out of a school notebook, lying in the center of the bedroom chair.

Dear Madeline,

I've never known anyone like you before, nor any people like your family either. You guys are all amazing—your openness and energy for one another, your devotion, the intensity with which you communicate and love each other. I have truly never seen this before. Frankly, it makes me incredibly uncomfortable. I need a break. You guys are awesome, but it's all a little much for me. You may have noticed that my stuff is gone; I'm going to hang out with my family for a while and chill.

I'm really sorry for the abruptness of all this.

Love always,

Dan

Madeline's thoughts went like this:

*You son of a bitch, who asked you to MOVE IN HERE IN THE FIRST PLACE?*

*You asshole douche bag, WHO SAID YOU COULD LEAVE NOW?*

*Wait. Seriously?! You couldn't even wait until I was finished folding the laundry? You had to rush around and sneak out before I even came upstairs? You chicken shit slime bag coward, YOU COULDN'T EVEN FACE ME?*

And finally:

*LOVE ALWAYS?!?! YOU HAVE GOT TO BE FUCKING KIDDING ME. LOVE? ALWAYS?*

The turkey feather conversation with Savannah echoing in her head and Dan's note clutched in her hand, Madeline pictured a chain of events that would extend into an inevitable future: she would put the turkey feather back in its spot on the end table; Dan would want to return in a few days; but at some point, Dan would vanish—again—and this time for good. The feather would remain for some amount of time, sometimes striking Madeline as a lovely and poignant token of a person who had stood beside her at an enormously tough time, sometimes as a stabbing reminder of someone who was prone to vanishing and would live the entire rest of his life this way. The day would come when the feather no longer carried any particular meaning whatsoever. It would be detritus. It would be tossed into a large plastic garbage bag and get covered with coffee grounds and used tissues and eggshells and rotten leftovers. The bag would be hauled out to the alley, where it would be crushed together with other bags. On some Thursday, men would toss it into the back of a truck. It would be squished and compacted and compressed. It would be dust.

She glanced at Dan's note, not reading the words, but taking in a general impression of the handwriting, the pattern of the markings on a torn page of paper. She crumpled the note into a ball and tossed it haphazardly in the general direction of the chair where she had found it. Inhaling deeply, Madeline caught the exhilarating, still-fresh aroma of the delicious Christmas tree downstairs. No question Frasier fir was the way to go; it smelled as if it had been chopped down yesterday. She pictured the Brawny paper-towel guy, ax slung over one shoulder, wearing nothing but his flannel shirt, ancient jeans, and worn boots as he trudged through the powdery snow in search of her tree.

She would leave the tree up until after New Year's. Maybe another week after that. Taking down the Christmas tree struck Madeline as one of the saddest things in the world. Even when Jeff had been around, she had always done it herself. He insisted that he couldn't trust himself to stow away the ornaments that had been handed down from her mother's family, as well as those from her own childhood and from all the Christmases when John and Kate were little—although this had never been an issue when they decorated the tree each year and Jeff would dive into the tissue-wrapped treasures with childlike glee. So be it. Yet another year when she would pack up the tree alone. It allowed Madeline a degree of ceremony she would not have otherwise. Time when she could hold the oldest ornaments—the ones her mother had painstakingly dated, going back to 1919—and try to picture her long-dead mother as the gangly, sickly, big-eyed child that she had seen in photographs, carrying an equally skinny, frightened-looking doll everywhere she went.

Taking down a Christmas tree was like a death. The death of another year. Pack up and put away whatever was special or memorable or lasting. Throw away the rest. Turkey feather. Christmas tree.

*Perhaps,* Madeline thought, *perhaps I have lived long enough.*

It seemed to her that she had seen a great many Christmases. That around the tree had gathered so many, many people whose lives had touched hers and who were now gone. Like a long Dickens novel, where the sheer volume of characters who paraded through the pages was impossible to keep track of or comprehend.

When she eventually dragged this perfect tree out to the curb, leaving a trail of needles she would find herself sweeping up well into the summer, Dan would be gone, too. *I have had so many different lives. Different little universes, created one conversation cup of coffee glass of wine walk along the lake whispered tender words caresses orgasms at a time. One at a time, day after day, and a world is constructed. What was it Octavio Paz said?*

*if two kiss*
*the world changes, desires take flesh*
*thoughts take flesh, wings sprout*
*on the backs of the slave, the world is real—*

*Oh shit. I must be seriously stressed. Quotes are popping into my head. Bad sign.*

*No. No, no, nope. Bathetic, mawkish, maudlin—that's what I'm being. And, my personal favorite—lachrymose.* Sometimes Madeline was goddamn glad that she had spent part of one summer studying lists of words to expand her vocabulary. "Lachrymose," she let the word swirl around inside her before she spoke it aloud. It wasn't every day that you could find a reason to use one of your favorite words of all time, but when that opportunity presented itself...that was a banner day. That could turn a shit day right around.

Madeline mustered determined intent to quell the coming tears. She wiggled back and forth in a little dance and two-stepped her way around her bedroom. Carefully moving aside the freshly laundered pile of clothes, she proceeded to rip the sheets off her bed with a vengeance and then crumpled them into the smallest ball she could. She held the ball out in front of her as she descended the two flights of stairs to the washing machine—arms fully extended as if the sheets emanated a putrid, horrifying stench.

*Ha. I knew I saved this for a reason,* she thought, ripping open a sample packet of laundry detergent that had arrived in the mail ages ago. Tide with Odor Control. Guaranteed to eliminate the toughest laundry odors, it said. *Well, then, my detergent friend, be true to your word. Eliminate, eliminate. When I lay my weary little head down on my pillow tonight—alone, in my own bed—I don't want a single whiff, not one hint of a whiff, not a hair of a tinge of a mite of a pinch of a speck of a trace of a hint. Of Dan.*

The machine's lid sang out as it snapped closed, making a kind of symphony with the rushing water and the whistling of the hot water pipe.

Madeline decided to slam the lid again. It felt highly satisfying. But when the last reverberation fell silent, it was as if a little bit of the air had escaped from Madeline's inner balloon. Her footfalls up the stairs were slow and shuffling. There was no dance this time.

Madeline's intention was to put away the laundry. She swung open the side-by-side doors of the primitive armoire she used for her clothes. She ran her eyes up and down the stacks of folded items, back and forth across the three shelves. Her eyes locked onto one of the stacks and remained there, not because she saw anything in particular, but because she had been suddenly overcome by an exhaustion that neared paralysis. She left the cabinet doors open and lay down on the sheetless bed.

Her flat palm grazed the mattress pad, and with that gesture, an image: Dan. Also lying on his back, the two of them facing the ceiling, newborn Dylan, tightly swaddled and sound asleep between their two prone bodies. Their hands reaching toward one another, clasping.

Madeline leapt from the bed and threw open the door of the hall closet, tossing around years' worth of accumulated things, searching for something she was certain had been stashed there ever since Kate's first big camping trip—Febreze Mountain-fresh scent.

Madeline bounded back into the bedroom and went to work on the pillows, nearly soaking them with spray. Then the mattress itself.

*Out damn spot! Wait a minute,* Macbeth? *Shakespeare? I thinketh not. Waaayyyyy too literary. How about Elmore Leonard?* Get Shorty? *"FUCK YOU, FUCKBALL!"*

Madeline punched the numbers into her phone and said, "Ellie, do you have any Febreze?"

"OK, even coming from you, even under the circumstances of your current life, I consider this to be an extremely weird question," Ellie said.

"I only got about three-quarters of the mattress sprayed. I just need a little bit more. To finish." Madeline said.

"Huh. And the fact that you seem to think that random and creepy statement is some sort of explanation isn't making me feel any better." Ellie's voice turned sober. "Seriously, are you OK?"

"No," Madeline said. "Not even slightly OK."

## Chapter 36

*I **was** eight years old when my grandmother had a stroke. My mother, my brother, and I boarded a jet plane as soon as we could book one from Pittsburgh, Pennsylvania, to San Diego, California. My mother hoped to arrive in time to see her own mother while she was still "herself." I understood that my grandmother was expected to die.*

*I felt suspended in the clouds, floating in what seemed like a slow-motion journey through the heavens. But I knew that the plane was actually going very fast, that we were crossing the entire United States in a few short hours. I also knew that we might not be fast enough. I knew that we were in a race against my grandmother's remaining time. I thought about the possibility that she might die while we were up in the clouds, and I wondered if I might be able to see her, making her trip to heaven, if I concentrated very hard on the clouds.*

*When my mother returned from visiting her mother in the hospital the day we arrived, she gave a brief report about how much my grandmother seemed like "herself." A brief, dry-eyed report. When she returned from the hospital the following day, my mother said that my grandmother was no longer "herself." She said she wished she had taken my brother and me to visit the previous day. Now it was too late. She said this with somber efficiency and entirely dry eyes. My grandmother died later that same day. My mother described how her body would be flown to Washington, D.C., so she could be buried beside my long-dead grandfather, the naval captain, in Arlington National Cemetery. I knew this was where President John F. Kennedy had been buried ten months earlier. I knew he had soldiers who guarded his grave around the clock and something called an Eternal Flame. I would get to see these things, my mother said.*

*My mother never cried. Not once. Not when she told me that her mother had died, not during the funeral service, not during the graveside service when my grandmother's coffin was lowered into a gaping hole lined with a hideous carpet of fake grass. I kept looking at my mother out of the corner of my eye, searching for any sign of a tear.*

*There is a part of me, deep inside, that is crying all the time now.*

## Chapter 37

For much of that fall, Madeline's communications with Kate were limited to phone calls of three to five minutes' duration while Kate waited for the bus. Madeline would answer the phone with an exaggerated "Kate-eeeeeeeeeeeee" and wait for Kate's echoing response, "Mom-eeeeeeeeee." A rat-a-tat of rapid-fire, bullet-point life tidbits would invariably be halted abruptly by a loud *whoosh* that announced the bus's arrival. Kate would attempt to shout something along the lines of, "I gotta go! Love you...," which trailed into an abrupt silence. Not a lot of free time in the second year of medical school. Madeline could not wait for her beloved and wise daughter to arrive home for Christmas break.

Kate was a self-described Christmas elf. She loved the season—everything about it—and attacked festivity with energy and delight.

On the first morning Kate was home, Madeline sat bolt upright and fully awake—as she did every morning—just before seven and tiptoed down to the kitchen. As she calculated how much coffee to make for Claire and Savannah (neither of whom would drink it) and herself and Kate, she was surprised to hear Kate's cough coming from the back sunroom.

Madeline poked her head around the corner and said, "What are you doing up?"

"I always get up early. You know that," Kate responded.

"Yeah, but I mean, what are you *doing*? You look like you're doing something back there."

"I'm making some flash cards."

"Flash cards? For what? And by the way, how long have you been up? Without coffee, is my point."

"Since six. I figured I'd get up every morning at six and chip away at this. Didn't want to take the time to make coffee. I knew you'd get up and make it right around now. And see? I've already gotten an hour of work done."

"You always were an odd child."

"I know."

"Flash cards for what, her mother asked, knowing she may well be sorry," Madeline said.

"For the medical boards. You know. The Boards, her daughter responded," said Kate.

"Just how many cards are in that box, anyway?"

"A thousand," Kate said.

"A thousand. One thousand. Are you actually planning to make a thousand flash cards?"

"I have another box."

"If you were a different person that would be a really good joke."

"Don't you remember when I was an undergrad, and I used to study in the med library?" Kate asked. "Don't you remember me describing to you when those med students were studying for their boards? Jesus, that was terrifying! It scared the shit out of me! I was trying to mind my own business and study, when all around me people were completely losing their shit, a little bit more and a little bit more, every day. I remember this one guy just wandering around, shaking all over, just wandering. This other guy kept muttering to himself and twisting strands of his hair. And then chuckling! It was seriously like being in a zombie apocalypse."

"So, the flash cards ward off the zombiism? Is that a word? Zombiism?"

"I'm hoping. I figured I'd get a jump on this over the holiday break."

"Geez. Fun times. Ho, ho, ho."

"Besides, it gives me something to focus on, apart from the shit storm that's going on right in my own living room," Kate said as she snapped a blank card out of the box.

"Now, now, you just got home last night. Don't you think you might want to wait a little while, give yourself some time to experience the shit storm for yourself before you start getting all despondent?"

"Nope. Don't you think I've been listening to you all fall? I think I've heard enough."

"Well, there was quite a bit of bus noise and a generally high level of haste," Madeline said. "I wasn't sure how much of what I said was actually sinking in."

"You don't need a weatherman to know which way the wind blows. Didn't some old guy from your generation say that?"

"Yeah. Some old guy did." Madeline continued, "A thousand note cards. You know what that reminds me of?"

"Hmmm," said Kate, absentmindedly.

"The thousand paper cranes," Madeline said.

When Kate was in her second year of college, she had gotten very ill. She left a quickly scribbled Post-it note on her dorm room door, announcing that she had left school and gone home. It was serious, and Kate believed—with good reason—that she would most likely die.

When she and Madeline made a trip back to Kate's dorm room to gather some things, they walked in to the dazzling sight of one thousand origami paper cranes. Some had been hung together in long vertical strings suspended from the ceiling, while others were strung in banners, wing to wing and hung from wall to wall. The sight and the surprise of it were magical.

The students on Kate's dorm floor had gotten together, night after night, to fold cranes, until their number counted one thousand, and they could bestow their gift that, according to Japanese legend, would ensure great health and long life to the recipient.

"They're still in the basement, aren't they?" Madeline asked. "Do you think they can work a second time?"

"Mom," Kate said, with great gentleness, "this is way beyond paper cranes."

It was then that the front door opened. Madeline and Kate

turned to see Dan walking slowly toward them, his stocking cap held in his two hands, as if in atonement.

Kate looked down at the flash card in front of her and resumed writing. Without looking at him, she said, "You must be Dan. I've heard so much about you."

Whereas Claire and Dan took an immediate and deep liking to one another, relaxing easily into a never-ending stream of things to say, it could not have been more different when Kate and Dan laid eyes on one another for the first time. Like two feral cats in a midnight alley, their backs hunched up instantly while they circled one another from a skeptical distance, ready to hiss and claw.

One look at Dan, and Kate saw someone who had hurt her mother and was going to hurt her more. "So very much," Kate added.

One sniff of Kate's wariness told Dan that Madeline's daughter had none of the usual susceptibility to his charms. His jaw set against her, and he reverted to his South Side Chicago upbringing—fists held protectively in front of his face, ready to throw the knockout punch.

"Yeah," Dan said, "it's a pleasure to meet you, too, Kate."

## Chapter 38

*John* and Claire went back and forth—over the phone, via text, and in e-mails of varying lengths—about how to get John back from Boston. The good news was John had finagled a way to do an internship in Chicago in lieu of his final semester of music school, and he would be able to live with his wife once again. The bad news was this meant he and all of their mutual possessions still residing in Boston (including three chronically stressed-out, rescue cats) needed to find their way back to Chicago, just two short months after Claire had made her solo move there. And all of this had to be planned around John's last days to do everything needed to finish his degree while still in Boston, as well as Claire's schedule with two jobs—plus the full-time job of her family.

For about a week, Claire would dash into whatever room Madeline and Dan inhabited and plop down beside them. Among a general flurry of accompanying movements and gestures, Claire would say something like, "What do you think about me renting a U-Haul in Chicago, driving to Boston to help John pack up and move, and then driving back here together? I think the mileage charge might actually be less than the one-way drop-off charge." But before either Dan or Madeline could respond, Claire would jump up, again with a flurry of waving arms, and say, "Never mind! It'll never work! I can't take that much time off work. Let alone be gone from…you know…*here*." By the time Claire reached the final word of her sentence, she would be two rooms away and Madeline and Dan would still not have uttered one word.

This happened at least once each day.

One day Claire said, "There's no other option at all whatsoever except for me to fly out there, rent a truck in Boston, and drive back here with John." Madeline and Dan had become so accustomed to Claire's abrupt departures after these announcements that they simply stared at her, blankly and without speaking. "Well? Come on, you guys. What the hell is wrong with you; what do you think?"

All went according to plan, and the reunited couple arrived one week before Christmas. John had one suitcase full of clothes and his backpack. The remainder of the rented truck contained three cats, five bicycles, two banjos, two guitars, two bass guitars, various equipment for sound engineering, and a mountain of amplifiers.

The closets filled up. The storage rooms filled up. All the spaces under the eaves in John and Claire's living space filled up. And with John home for Christmas and for good, seven people went to sleep under Madeline's roof each night.

When Madeline descended the stairs the morning after his

return, John had set up one of his bikes on a stand in the living room, right between the piano and the Christmas tree. *Just like old times,* Madeline thought.

"Still on Boston time," John said. "Couldn't manage to sleep the extra hour. Hey, I couldn't really figure out any other place to set up a bike 'shop.' Is this OK with you?"

Madeline did a quick survey of the open toolboxes—two of them—and the assortment of wrenches, bolts, screws, and general whatnots strewn across much of the floor. "Of course," she said.

"No, I mean, I knew you were going to say yes, but is it really OK?"

"Yes," Madeline said. "Really, really."

*My beautiful baby boy,* Madeline thought. "You are all growed up," she said.

"Well, sort of," John said, gesturing to the surrounding rubble with his wrench.

*What a crazy thing,* Madeline thought. *You bring these little tiny people into the world; you care for them day and night, day after day. You love them with a power and a ferocity you never could have imagined, and you would move worlds to protect them from pain. You do this for years and years. And then you let them go. You watch them live their own lives. But from a greater and greater distance, because this is the way it is supposed to be.*

Madeline was transported years into the past. John had just come home from his day at high school. He took the gallon of milk from the refrigerator, hoisted himself to sit on the kitchen counter, and removed the cap to drink it straight from the jug. "Mom," he said to Madeline, "will you make me a PB&J?"

She had regarded the six-foot man-child in front of her, torn between her feeling that perhaps a good parent would chastise John for drinking straight from the milk jug, or would a good parent let it go knowing that John was the only one who drank whole milk in the first place?

"Please," he added, and the sheepish, ironic expression on his face told her he knew this was an unreasonable request for an eighteen-year-old, yet he relished making it. "Yours are always better than when I make them. Yours are the best."

Sometimes you have no idea, none at all, which of the simplest, most everyday, completely unexceptional moments might become emblazoned in your mind for the rest of time. A snapshot of an instance, a place in your life that remains in extraordinary, vivid detail—no blurring around the edges of a picture that never fades. Other times, you do know. Madeline knew, right then and there, that the peanut butter sandwich request was one of the moments she would remember.

## Chapter 39

*I*t was long past the time when Madeline would make an entire village of gingerbread houses for each room of the house's first floor—gumdrop streets lined with gingerbread men and women, M&M rooftops with chocolate Santas waving from chimneys, forests of festooned trees, and front yards with cheery snowmen. *Still,* she thought to herself, *this Christmas will not be a shit show. It can't be.*

Christmas Eve had always been Madeline's favorite part of the entire holiday season. The calendar had wound down relentlessly to the shortest days of the year, the barest amount of daytime to illuminate a bleak winter landscape; yet this day seemed to stretch out—timelessly—with the bright promise of going on forever, like a day in the middle of July.

Dan had drifted off to spend some time with his family. Savannah had been holed up at her Aunt Carol's with Dylan for several days, and Claire had left early in the morning to join them. The only ones in the house that morning were Madeline and her two children.

Madeline was finishing the frosting on the Christmas tree–shaped cakes that had been an unbreakable tradition for years. The tin foil pans had likely been designed for one-time-then-toss-them use. About twenty years ago. Each year Madeline consulted her kids for Christmas Eve menu planning. Each year she asked them what they wanted for dessert. With cheery overenthusiasm, she would mention a few yummy possibilities she'd been wanting to make for them. Even if the two of them were on the phone, Madeline could hear Kate's face fall; she could imagine the tears that threatened at the corner of Kate's eyes at the mere idea of a change. Each year Madeline babied the weary pans into shapes that reasonably resembled Christmas trees and filled the ever-expanding holes with scraps of aluminum foil so they had a fair chance of holding the batter.

Madeline hummed a medley of carols as she swirled the finishing touches of bright green frosting. She imagined the conversation that was about to take place:

"OK, guys, the cakes are ready for you to decorate!"

"Come on, John!" Kate would say.

"You do both of them this year, Kate. I'm in the middle of trying to finish this (fill-in-the-blank, critically important thing)," John would say.

"No, no, no, no, no, no. Come on! It's your cake! *Your cake!*"

This would go on for a bit, John resisting, Kate getting increasingly filled with flustered affectionate pique.

In the end, John would create a masterpiece in a blindingly short amount of time. Kate would study, plan, and go back to her work again and again for fine-tuning. Ultimately, they would both be so pleased with their work that they would carve and gouge around their favorite bits of cake decoration, until they were the last few bites that remained on the platter.

Before Madeline could call out to signal she had completed her final flourishes, and right in the transition between her humming of "Silent Night" and "O Holy Night," the sounds of Kate and John tuning up their instruments in the living room drifted in. "Yeah!" she said.

"Surprise!" shouted Kate. "Impromptu Christmas carol serenade!"

Madeline walked into the living room with a knife full of frosting still in hand, holding it out first to Kate, then to John, as they plucked strings and turned pegs to tune.

"Let's do 'O Holy Night' first 'cause it's my favorite, and Mom was just about to sing it," Kate said.

"OK," John replied. "I don't really know it, so you start, and I'll come in and follow."

"What do you mean, you don't know 'O Holy Night'? That's, like, blasphemy or something," Kate said.

"Are we gonna have this conversation again?" John asked.

Madeline plopped onto the couch, happier than she could remember being in a long, long time.

"I suppose I should think about starting to get dinner ready. Did Claire give you any idea what time she'd be back here?"

"Um, I'm not sure she's gonna make it back for dinner," John did his best to sound casual, but his head remained turned away, his eyes on the floor as he answered his mother.

"What do you mean?" Madeline's voice was nearly a whisper.

"I don't think things are going so well. At Aunt Carol's. I don't think anybody's in a very good mood."

"What's going on, John?"

John sank into a chair and ran his fingers through his hair, still looking at some point on the floor, then at the ceiling. He combed his fingers through his hair a few more times and let out a big, audible puff of breath. "I guess I mean that Savannah's really, really down, so Claire is really down, too. Because her sister is. You know?"

"What's up with Savannah?"

"She's spent all this time out there with Aunt Carol thinking about how it's Dylan's first Christmas and how important that is, and, well, she got more and more convinced that her mother was going to be able to get it together and have Christmas with all of them."

"Oh, shit," Madeline said.

"Yeah," said John.

"Shit."

"Yeah."

"Well, what's happening now?" Madeline asked.

"I don't know. Savannah was just so *sure* that Billie would show up. Every day since she left here, I guess she's gotten her hopes more and more wound up. Everybody has been calling Billie all day long—they started this morning—and she hasn't answered. They've texted about a hundred times, too. Anyway, finally Uncle Bob drove down there because Carol was losing her mind not knowing what was going on with her sister. So Bob gets down there and the apartment is totally dark. No lights. No nothing."

"Oh, no," Madeline said. "Oh my God, poor Carol and Bob."

"Yeah," John said. "The poor guy was walking around outside of Billie's apartment peeking in the windows and tapping on the glass. On Christmas Eve. Anyway, when he got back home, Savannah crashed and burned. She got really, really down and went pale and handed Dylan over to Claire and locked herself in a bedroom. Hasn't come out or said a word since then."

Kate looked John square in the eye and said, "Do you want to play a few more tunes or go decorate the cakes now?"

John met her stare and held it. "So like I said, I don't think anybody out there is in a very good mood."

"Seems like that would be an understatement," said Madeline.

"Claire is trying to talk Savannah into packing up Dylan and coming here. But I don't know if that's gonna happen," John said.

"Well, what should I do about dinner? Should I hold off starting to cook?"

"No, don't hold off," Kate broke in. "We told them what time dinner was going to be."

Both Madeline and John looked at her. "It's Christmas Eve!" Kate said. "If they make it for dinner—great. If not, they'll be here later on."

"Well," Madeline said, "looks like it may be just the three of us for dinner!" Her children knew her well enough to glean the mostly disguised elation in her voice.

"Make a lot of food anyway, Ma. Please? They might be hungry when they get here."

"*If* they get here," Kate said, with unapologetic accuracy.

Madeline, John, and Kate were the only three people sitting around the dinner table for their traditional Christmas Eve feast.

"Oh my God, this is so good, Mom. I'm gonna get a little more and then roll around on the floor in front of the fire and groan in discomfort, and it will be so worth it," Kate said.

"Hey, leave some for Claire. She said they're on their way," said John.

"Didn't they have a big, giant dinner at Carol's? Wasn't that the whole idea—a big family dinner where Billie could show up? Slip in and out?" Kate asked.

"Still. I want her to have some of our dinner. It'll be sort of like she was here. With me. With all of us."

"Oh, sweetie. I'm so sorry Claire wasn't here," Madeline said.

"She will be," John replied.

## Chapter 40

*Kate* proved true to her prediction. She was, in fact, lying on the living room floor in front of the fire—her feet resting on top of an ottoman while she rubbed her belly and let out the occasional contented groan—when Claire and Savannah came through Madeline's front door. They entered without making a sound. At first their faces lacked any discernible expressions. It was Claire who carried baby Dylan in his front-pack carrier. *Crap,* Madeline thought, *I'm guessing that means a world of shit.*

Savannah sank into the chair closest to the door. She did not remove her coat. It bunched up around her neck when she sat, throwing her hair into wild disarray. She made no attempt to move the hair that had fallen in front of her face. Madeline glanced at Savannah and thought: *It's slumped. Her very* face *is slumped. I didn't know such a thing was possible.* Savannah managed to radiate jaw-clenched, seething malcontent like waves carrying forth from an ocean liner. It was impossible to be in the room, which was quite large, and not know the intense level of her suffering.

Madeline's phone rang in the other room. When she saw the name on her caller ID, she walked to the back of the house to answer. "Hi," she said.

"Don't tell anyone that it's me. Please. Please, Maddie." Billie's voice was so soft, so nearly not there at all.

"What's going on, Billie? How are you?"

Billie cried quietly on the other end of the line for quite a while. "I am so sorry, Maddie. So, so sorry. I've let everybody down. Again. I've let everybody down again."

"Everybody wants you here," was Madeline's first lie. "But everybody understands," was her second.

Billie's gentle crying turned to great, racking sobs; she audibly snorted the torrent of liquid that poured from her nose. "I just can't do it. I can't. I can't, I can't, I can't."

"Are you OK, Billie? Are you someplace safe?"

"I can't, I can't, I can't. I'm so, so sorry."

"Your sister is worried about you. Can you call her? Or text her? Can you text Savannah? Wish her a good Christmas? Can you think about doing that? At least before the end of the day tomorrow. Just think about it. Please just think about it, OK?"

"Don't tell anyone I called," Billie said and abruptly hung up.

Madeline remained in the back room, weighing the pros and cons of keeping the call to herself. *Talk about your lose-lose,* she thought. *Claire counts on knowing every single thing about her mother, all the time, even when the information makes her completely miserable.*

Just then, Claire stealthed into the room and said to Madeline, "Who was that? Was that my mother?"

"I'm not sure," Madeline replied. "Depends on: what's the right answer to that question?"

"Goddamn it!" Claire said. "What did she say?"

"Not much. She doesn't sound good. I think it's a safe bet that we won't be seeing her. I tried to get her to think about talking to her sister...and to Savannah."

"Where is she? What else did she say?"

"She didn't say much, Claire. Mostly she cried. Hard. And repeatedly apologized. Repeatedly."

The two women looked at one another across the dark expanse of the room and said nothing. Claire retreated, leaving Madeline to gaze out at the backyard, the fat colored lights ablaze in the neighbor's tall pine.

Right after Madeline returned to the living room and took her seat on the couch, the front door opened, and Dan came in. *Fuck, I should have expected this,* Madeline thought. She knew well that any time Dan spent with his family entailed heavy drinking on Dan's part. Not until he walked through the door did Madeline realize it: she had held out the hope that Christmas Eve would be different, that maybe there would be warmth and traditions and laughter and such that would have him sipping daintily at a homemade toddy instead of slugging back a large number of brews.

Dan perplexed her when he drank. Alcohol seemed to render him both woozy and intense. There was a coiled-snake vibe, ready at any second to strike, hard, unless he happened to slip into a peaceful stupor instead. He plopped onto the couch next to her, but sat at the very edge, so he needed to turn most of the way around to see Madeline. "Wow," he said, "look at this cozy family scene."

"Yep," Madeline said. "It is." It was both a command and a plea.

"Cozy, cozy," Dan snarled.

## Chapter 41

*Early* Christmas morning, Kate found her mother in the kitchen, babysitting the coffee pot as it burbled away.

"Mama! Merry Christmas!" She threw her arms around Madeline and said simultaneously: "Don't even think about touching that pot until it's all done."

"Oh, for God's sake, I do this every morning! Every morning I pour myself a cup. That's why there is such a thing as stop-and-pour. So we don't have to wait! So civilization can march forward!"

"It will totally ruin the rest of the pot. No touch."

"On this of all days! It's Christmas. Mama needs her coffee!"

Kate decided it was easier to simply place herself between her mother and the brewing pot.

"You're a terrible human being," Madeline said.

"Stockings first? Same as ever? Then breakfast?"

"Of course," Madeline replied. "Same as ever. Oh, no! Shit! I didn't even think about a stocking for Savannah. Didn't even enter my head! Assuming she comes out of her room. At all."

"Of course Savannah has a stocking," Kate said. "Santa would never forget Savannah."

"Oh my God," Madeline said. "Oh my God."

"I forgot, too. Until the middle of the night."

"What did you do?" her mother asked.

"Go look," Kate said. "I thought I was going to have to use one of those nasty ones you've kept all these years from your childhood—even though that creepy angel keeps losing more and more parts of her body like some pathetic leper—but anyway, there was a pretty new one in the box, too. Do you even remember why we got that one? I had to empty out all of the stockings, dig through everything, and then take a little bit from everybody else's stocking. Even my own. Sorry. Most of the stuff, though, I had to take from your stocking. Things I got for you. I think it will be OK. It's not totally even, but I think it'll be OK."

"Oh my God, Kate, that's amazing. You're amazing." Madeline teared up and hurtled toward Kate with outstretched arms, intending an enormous hug. But Kate took a step backward.

"Not that I expect it will make any difference. But I thought I would try. I thought somebody should at least try."

Gathering five adults, a teen mother, and a newborn baby in one room long enough to reach in and pull out painstakingly chosen treasures from Madeline's hand-knit Christmas stockings proved to be a challenging mission. Pots of coffee were brewed and drained, favorite Christmas CDs from years long past rang out on the stereo one after another—and still, no more than four people at a time managed to gather in the general vicinity of the tree, the stockings, and the waiting piles of gifts.

The only person in unfettered good spirits was baby Dylan. As a one-month-old who had every reason to express general difficulty in his adjustment to the whole world outside of a warm, dark, wholly embracing womb, he rarely did. The bright lights, noise, and general chaos that he had been born into seemed to fascinate and delight him. Madeline regularly said to Savannah, "He's not a real baby, you know." Savannah, of course, had nothing to compare him to. She had no idea that sleepless nights were the norm, instead of an infant who nestled into his mother's ample chest and snoozed the night away.

Kate planted herself in the living room, turned off the Mormon Tabernacle Choir mid-carol, and opened her violin case. "John," she shot over her shoulder, "let's play until everyone's here."

"I was just—" John said.

"Let's play." Kate's breathing was faster than usual.

John wandered back and forth in the room, as if trying to remember what her words meant.

"Oh, great!" Madeline said, rushing into the room and plopping down on the sofa. "Best idea ever. More impromptu carols!" She knit her brow and continued, "Hey, anybody seen Dan? What the heck is he doing?"

"What the fuck is *anybody* doing," Kate said. "Seriously, what the fuck is everybody doing?"

"Dan," Madeline called out. "DAN!"

A door on the second floor opened. "Yeah?" Dan said.

"Hey, can you come down here?" Madeline asked.

With a few tentative footfalls on the staircase, Dan stood on the landing. Uncommitted to the remaining six stairs, he looked at Madeline with mildly annoyed bewilderment.

"Whatcha doing up there?" Madeline inquired.

Dan shrugged.

"Well, come down and sit with me," Madeline said. "Listen to the kids with me. Come on."

Dan padded down the remaining steps and took his place beside Madeline. "Here? You want me here? Like this?"

"Hey, what's up with you?" Madeline asked.

"Nothing. Here I am."

"Oh my God," said Kate. "We actually have four people here. All we need is Claire and Savannah."

"I'm pretty sure Claire's in the basement. On the phone or texting someone. Savannah's upstairs. Also on the phone."

"Let me know the next time and place that my services are required," Dan said, standing.

"No, no, no, no!" Madeline said. "Stay here! I'm gonna see if I can rally the troops."

"I'm around. Once the troops get rallied, let me know," Dan countered.

"Hey! Come on! This is fun!" Madeline said.

"Do you know the *New Yorker* cartoonist Roz Chast?" Dan asked.

"Yeah…," said Madeline.

"Cartoon title: 'Pollyanna in Hell.' Cartoon caption: 'No more down jackets forever!!!' "

Madeline made an excellent attempt to shoot daggers with her glance, but Dan refused to meet her gaze as he left the room and climbed the stairs.

Madeline heard her phone's tone that announced an incoming text.

Auggie: Bess and I send all our love for a festive family Christmas!

Madeline: Hey! Merry Christmas, you guys!

Auggie: How's it going there?

Madeline: Hahaha. "Herding cats" doesn't even begin to cover it. The word "travesty" might come close.

Auggie: We love you, Madeline! Can't wait for all the gory details.

Madeline: The really gory detail is how I turned out to be a hopelessly shallow person who fell for a handsome lunatic.

Bess: Bess here. Was reading over Auggie's shoulder. Merry Christmas!

Madeline: To you, too!

Bess: Don't be so hard on yourself. No one deserved a fling with an underwear model more than you.

Madeline: Lunatic underwear model. Also, sad to say, bad person.

Bess: Ah, crap. I'm sorry.

Madeline: I wanted your ending. The Auggie and Bess happy ending.

Bess: I know, I know. We're right up the street.

Madeline: When the dust settles...if the dust settles...you can help me try to locate my self-esteem.

Bess: Right up the street. Ready to do whatever you need.

Madeline: Sigh. Thanks. So much.

Bess: Gotta run. Auggie is blowing kisses at the phone.

With much time, and even more cajoling, six people eventually gathered in Madeline's living room in front of a roaring fire. Kate donned the traditional Santa Claus hat and placed each person's Christmas stocking in his or her lap. Looking around the Christmas morning stocking circle, Madeline thought: *I'm in the Twilight Zone, some sort of twisted parallel universe. It's like a crazy improv class where each person has been given an exaggerated character trait that they're supposed to act out, and they're supposed to hang onto that trait for dear life, no matter what anyone else might be doing.*

The exaggerated traits went as follows:

Savannah: I WILL sulk, pout, sigh, disappear at regular intervals, and broadcast dark despair.

Claire: I WILL stick with Savannah. This is blood. If she's in despair, I'm in despair. Don't fuck with me.

John: I WILL remain completely oblivious to anything out of the ordinary going on here. Completely. Oblivious.

Kate: I WILL HAVE A GOOD CHRISTMAS. I WILL. I WILL. I WILL.

Dan: I WILL act as if every single thing this family has created as part of their Christmas tradition is without question the most fucked up, lame-assed, terrifyingly inauthentic piece of dysfunctional lunacy that I have ever witnessed in my life.

Madeline: I WILL do everything humanly possible to make

sure that each and every one of these people is happy, happy, happy. I can do it! I can!

"Oh, look, another piece of chocolate," Savannah said, tossing it onto the end table.

From the time that John and Kate were babies, the tradition had been for each member of the family to pull one thing at a time out of his or her stocking, taking turns from the youngest to the oldest, until each stocking had been emptied, and each individual item oohed and aahed over with great ceremony.

Claire had spent enough Christmas mornings with John's family to have already gone through her various stages and mixtures of bafflement, horrified worry, warm and fuzzy charmed, bemused detachment, and, ultimately, acceptance of a quaint foreign culture's deeply entrenched and mysterious ways.

Savannah, on the other hand, coming into the Stocking Circle for the first time, was purely and simply pissed.

Kate, being the second youngest, followed Savannah. "Oh my God! Look at this! I forgot all about this kind of candy! We used to get this all the time when we were kids! I didn't think they made this anymore. I wonder where in the world Santa found this!"

"Santa has his ways," Madeline said. "We do not question the ways of Santa." She added, "But I'm sure Santa knows how tickled you are, and that—"

"Oh look, yet *another* little piece of chocolate," Savannah held up a chocolate truffle that was a beloved family favorite.

Madeline and Kate whipped their heads around, voices

overlapping as they both said, “Savannah! It’s *not your turn!*”

“What!?” Savannah said.

“We explained this to you,” Kate said. “We take turns. One person at a time, one thing from the stocking at a time. Youngest to oldest!”

Savannah looked back and forth between Kate and Madeline, her mouth slightly open, her expression that of someone who is searching for an explanation, for some meaning that is utterly escaping her.

“Right,” Savannah said. Then, “You guys are weirdos.”

“You’re a weirdo,” said Claire.

*Bless her little heart,* thought Madeline. *Bless her, bless her, bless her. She’s trying to get her sister on board.*

“No, you’re a weirdo,” Savannah said, sinking against the back of her chair. She tossed the truffle on the table and let out a very pronounced sigh.

“Whose turn is it?” Madeline said. “Come on, we could all starve to death before breakfast at this rate.”

“Well, we have more people!” Claire said. “Maybe we should just…take all the stuff out of our stockings…all at once…because we have more people…you know?”

“It’s not going to take *that* long,” said Kate.

“So…one at a time then…?” Claire said, looking to Madeline and John.

“It’s not going to take that long,” Kate repeated.

Savannah let out another very pronounced sigh.

“Hey, John, did you finish off all the beer from last night?” Dan asked.

"Very funny, Dan," Madeline said.

As soon as the stockings had been emptied, family members scattered once again. Savannah grabbed her phone and withdrew to her bedroom. Claire grabbed her phone and retreated to the basement. Dan simply disengaged, removing himself to a room where he could sit alone. The earlier difficulty of gathering everyone for stockings repeated itself with the new effort to assemble everyone for Christmas breakfast.

Claire emerged from the basement and into the kitchen where Kate and Madeline were preparing breakfast. "Savannah's not coming down for breakfast," Claire said.

Kate spun around from the stove and said, "Oh, for Christ's sake, are you and Savannah texting each other from inside the fucking house?"

Claire's face hardened, and she addressed herself solely to Madeline. "You should go ahead without us. Savannah and I are skipping breakfast."

"Wait, *what?*" Kate said, and immediately switched from irritation to entreaty. "No, really, Claire, *please* have breakfast with us. I'm asking you. Please."

The two young women stared at one another for a moment. Claire said, "All right. I'll sit with you all at the table. But I'm not going to eat anything."

Within seconds of Claire's butt hitting the dining room chair, Dan jumped up from his seat and said, "The coffee's probably nearly ready. Anybody else?"

"Seriously?" Kate said. "We *just* sat down. Finally! We finally all sat down."

"Be right back," Dan said.

The ornery coffeepot chose that exact moment to erupt. Rivulets of grainy, blackish brew ran in multiple directions across the kitchen countertops, into the crack between the counter and the stove, down the cabinets, and across the floor.

"Shit," said Dan. "Total explosion."

"You're fucking kidding me," Madeline said, leaping to her feet. "I'm coming."

"Mom, please stay here. Please." The barely contained flood of tears soaked Kate's voice.

"No, she's right," Dan said. "I got this." Though he continued to stand motionless, holding a dish towel and staring blankly at the outpouring before him.

"Dan, can you come back in here, too? Please can you come in here? Can we all just sit here, together, at the breakfast table for a few minutes?" Kate implored.

Dan did not respond, and Kate turned to her mother, "Can you ask him? Can you please get him to just come sit down?"

Without hesitation, Madeline turned in her chair and faced into the kitchen. "Dan. Please. I'll clean it up later. Just leave it. Please come sit down."

The house held its breath. Dan took a long time to put the towel on the kitchen counter. Slowly he walked the few steps into the dining room, pulled out a chair, and sat at the head of the table, folding his hands in front of him. No one moved.

Kate picked up her fork to resume Christmas breakfast, and,

with that, Dan shoved himself back in his chair and spit in a low, tightly coiled whisper: "Do you feel better now, Kate? Do you feel better now that you've ordered everyone around and gotten exactly what you wanted? Even though it's fucking crazy? It's fucking crazy that there's coffee spilling all over the kitchen, but you got what you wanted."

Kate exploded into tears, exploded out of her chair, exploded from the room at a gallop, her mother a hair's breadth of explosion behind her, reaching out her arms and calling her daughter's name.

The house split in two. In one part, two women raced through the living room and tore up the stairway in a tumult of noise and limbs and sobs and entreaties. In the other part, three people sat in motionless silence, their eyes locked to their laps.

"Can I come in?" Madeline implored from outside Kate's bedroom door. "Please, Kate."

There was no response, just the heart-shredding, choking sobs on the other side. Madeline knocked hard and fast. When there was no answer, she knocked again, as gently as a whisper. "Will you please talk to me? Can I come in for one second?"

"No."

"OK, I won't come in then. Will you talk to me from there?"

"Please just go away," Kate said at last. "Now. I need you to go away. I need to be by myself."

"Honey...are you sure? Are you sure it's not better for me to...just give you...a hug? Then I'll go?"

"Mom," was all Kate said.

"Ok," Madeline responded. "All right. I'm going."

Madeline wrenched herself from Kate's door, with silent steps backward, still facing the door and the minuscule possibility that Kate might change her mind and come flying out of her room and into her mother's waiting arms.

When Madeline had backed her way to the top of the staircase, she encountered Dan on his way up. He passed her without a word and went into her bedroom. She watched as he retrieved his ludicrously over-used grocery bag and tossed his things into it.

"What's the plan, Dan?"

"Leaving," Dan said.

"Leaving?" Madeline said. "Again?" And then, "Seriously? *Again?*"

*I've turned into a batshit lunatic,* Madeline thought. *For all the times I've wanted to tell him never to darken my doorway again, I don't want* him *to be the one who gets to decide. Batshit!*

Dan brushed passed Madeline once more, on his way to the back bathroom, where he opened the medicine cabinet and tossed his toothbrush into the bag. And then his floss.

"Oh dear, this is serious, I see," said Madeline. "He has the floss!" Their eyes locked for a split second of pure hate, then Madeline's softened. "Dan, seriously, where are you going? *Why* are you going?"

"Someplace else," he said. "Any place else."

With Kate behind the closed door of one bedroom, and Savannah holed up with baby Dylan behind the door of another, Madeline dropped her voice to a seething whisper as she faced Dan in the hallway. "You realize you were *invited* to Christmas here, right? By me, by my whole family. We all wanted you here. And you said that you wanted to be here."

"Obviously a mistake," Dan snarled. "This is fucking crazy. *You* are fucking crazy."

"Crazy? Crazy!" Madeline said, expectorating great bursts of spit and air in her effort to make her point while remaining hushed, and all the while waving her arms wildly, seeming very much like, well, a crazy lunatic. "This is a family, Dan. Families *are* crazy. Sometimes. But you know what families do? Dan? They stick around." *They fucking stick around. They don't throw a bunch of shit in a little brown bag and take off every time things get hard. That's what they don't fucking do.*

"It's not my family, Madeline."

"Yeah, I'm aware of that," Madeline said. *Except you do the same thing with your own family. With everyone. You invite yourself in. You stay for as long as you're charmed and entertained. Then you leave. You move on. Then you do it again.*

Dan said nothing.

*And again and again! You bogus Buddhist, self-absorbed, floss-fetishistic prick!*

"Your life isn't for everyone, Madeline," Dan said.

"What the fuck is that supposed to mean?"

"It means that your life isn't for everyone. The closeness. The force of the love," Dan said.

"Gosh, that does sound awful," snarked Madeline.

"You sucked me in!" Dan said. "But…it's too much. It's just… way too much."

*I sucked you in! Who showed up with their brown paper bag and said he couldn't imagine being anywhere else blah, blah, blah, and he wanted to cook for me blah, blah, blah, and it was my turn to be taken care of, my turn,* MY TURN *blah, blah,* BULLSHIT*!* "It's life, Dan. You're essentially saying that life is too much."

"Well," Dan countered, "sometimes it is."

*Liar! You fucking lied. And I fucking believed you! I was stupid enough...lonely enough...that I let you lick my wounds!* "Wow," Madeline said, "and you're the one jetting off to some tropical paradise to study meditation. To find compassion. Isn't that what you've said—find compassion?"

Dan sighed heavily. "I'm leaving, Madeline. You guys are all crazy."

"Good fucking luck with the compassion thing," Madeline said, and then she repeated it at a much higher volume: "GOOD FUCKING LUCK WITH THE COMPASSION THING."

Madeline watched Dan's gorgeous back descend the stairs. She remained at the top, the closed doors of Kate's room and Savannah's room still presenting their inscrutable faces. A slight rustling of fabric suggested that Dan was putting on his coat. The front door knob grazed the radiator with a dull metal thump, announcing what Madeline imagined was Dan's departure.

The thump led to a wellspring of action downstairs. John and Claire shot out of their dining room chairs to see who might be coming or going, then burst out the front door once they surmised the obvious sum of two plus two. Through the window, Madeline watched her son and his wife jog coatless through the frosty Christmas morning, trying to reach Dan before he drove off in his car.

*Like watching a movie with the sound turned off,* Madeline thought. She felt a strange detachment, as if the people before her could be anyone; their story could be anything. Even with the distance, though, Madeline could see Dan in the driver's seat—motionless, looking down—avoiding the eyes of the two people approaching his car. John stood directly in front of the car, as if to block it, while Claire banged on the window. Dan raised his head, looking from one to the other. When Claire raised her arms in a "what gives?" shrug, Dan opened the car door and got out.

The three of them stood carefully apart from one another. Madeline could see their mouths moving, the vapor from their breath condensing into clouds of fog and disappearing into thin air, as if the words themselves had been nothing at all. Not until Claire threw her arms around Dan did it occur to Madeline: it was entirely likely that she would never see Dan again. As she watched John bear-hug Dan and thwack him on the back, a pang shot through her. *How utterly bizarre,* she thought, *that one of the people I have been closest to during these past four months may have just left my life. Forever.*

Every fingernails-on-a-chalkboard moment of the past weeks raced through her head, as she recollected the depth of her wishing him gone. But, the other side was there as well: Madeline felt the black, gnawing hole of his absence tearing at the edges—the lack of warmth beside her in bed, the hand no longer holding her own, the companionship no longer there. She would once again do battle with loneliness.

Shivering and downtrodden, Claire and John returned to the house. Madeline greeted them at the door. "Scrabble, anyone?"

"Sorry, Mom," John said.

Madeline said nothing.

Claire threw her arms around Madeline in a ferocious, enveloping hug.

"Sorry he turned out to be kind of a dick," John added, putting his own arms around his wife and his mother.

"Kind of," said Madeline, with dripping irony.

"I'm sure if I'd gotten to know him better, I'd be able to say that he was a complete dick," John said.

Madeline laughed, a small but genuine laugh, and wiped away a tear. "Thanks, honey."

"You know, it can be hard to come into this family from the outside," Claire said. "Especially at Christmas."

Madeline looked at Claire. "You don't like the way we do Christmas? I always thought you did."

"No, I do. I do!" Claire said, looking to John.

"We can be pretty intense, Mom. We have our ways of doing things. Which is great. But it doesn't allow for much...flexibility," John said.

John's solidness, his gentleness, moved Madeline deeply. She looked back and forth between her son and Claire and said, "Sounds like the two of you have been talking about this."

"Our traditions have been great...but...we've never changed

*anything.* Never made room for anything new, or different. Or anyone."

"But we invited Dan to be with *our* family, for *our* Christmas. You don't just show up at someone else's holiday and trash it —act like every single thing they do is shit!" Madeline said.

"But our Christmas now is different than our Christmas used to be," John said. "I mean, jeez, look around, pretty much everything is different. I'm just saying—maybe we could be a little more...adaptable."

"Are you on *his* side here?" Madeline snipped.

"Jesus, Mom, no! Plus, there aren't sides!"

"Of course there are!" Madeline said, at which point she broke into an open-mouthed cackle, a loud laugh that spanned the range from self-effacement to unbridled mirth to barely suppressed hysteria.

John and Claire were taken aback.

"Were you serious about Scrabble?" Claire asked.

"No," Madeline said. "Well, yes. Maybe. What I'm serious about is getting Kate out of her room before this day is over."

"It's a worthy goal, but it may not happen," John said. "*She's* the one who needs everything to stay the same, Mom. You know that, right? You go along with it because you take all your cues from her."

"Give her a fucking break, John. She lost her dad. She lost her picture of a family. She thought she was going to fucking die. This is really important to her," Madeline replied.

"I know she thought that! Jesus, of course I know. But it's been...it was all a pretty long time ago," John said.

"Give her time," Madeline said. "She'll move ahead on her own, when she's ready."

"Or maybe she won't. Maybe she needs us to show her how," John said. "Dad's still alive, Mom. Kate was the one who banished him until New Year's so she could keep all the traditions completely intact. I mean, sheesh."

As if on cue, Kate flung open the door of her room and yelled from the top of the stairs, "Who's up for a movie? *The Hobbit* or *Monsters, Inc.*? I vote for *The Hobbit.*"

Savannah burst from behind her own door and said, "I'm totally in. I don't even care what we see."

"Race you down the stairs," Kate said.

Recognizing a tenuous and fragile crack in the clouds, but a crack nonetheless, Claire ran around gathering hats and coats and scarves and gloves while saying, "Let's not even check the show times. Let's just go to the theater. Now."

"Come on, Mom," John said. "Come with us."

"Well," said Madeline, "I think someone should stay here."

"Why? You should come!"

"Yeah! Get out of the house!"

"Come on!"

Madeline watched the flurry of garments being donned, then said, "I was thinking someone should stay here because… because there's a one-month-old baby asleep upstairs."

"Oh, shit," Savannah said.

## Chapter 42

*My mother loved to tell the story of when I was sick with the chicken pox. I came downstairs in my pajamas, miserable with pain and itch, wretched with a high fever. I stood in the kitchen and cried.*

*Our beloved family dog Heidi had recently given birth to a litter of eight tiny, squiggling black puppies. In anticipation, my father had built her a small pen in our basement and filled it with old blankets, so she would have a place to birth and then raise her pups.*

*When Heidi heard my sobs, she left her pups in their basement pen and came up to see the situation for herself. My mother never stopped delighting in telling how Heidi nuzzled into me and began giving me gentle but insistent pushes toward the basement staircase. She was trying to herd me down the stairs, so I could join the rest of the babies that needed her.*

*While Heidi did love me best of our family of four, I thought it was mighty generous of my mother to say so, and to delight in it, considering that she had done the lion's share of the hard work of housebreaking and training and feeding and slogging the big dog inside and outside since the day we had brought her home. I was three years old then and therefore instantly and deeply in love. I held the sleeping puppy for hours. I examined every square inch of her as she grew, so I would know her dog body as well as I could. Until the very end of her life, whenever I would sit on the floor in front of a heating vent in order to shake off winter's chill, she would lie down next to me, resting her head in my lap. I spread her ears out across my thigh and stroked them, reveling in their unequaled softness.*

*I have no memory of the chicken pox incident myself, but I heard it so many times growing up that I have formed a clear picture of it—Heidi's expression of alertness and concern, my flannel pajamas with faded yellow flowers all over them, so small on me that my five-year-old belly showed in the space between the tops and the bottoms. My only memory of the chicken pox was watching my mother pour nearly a full box of cornstarch into a steaming hot bath and telling me that it would help with the terrible itching. It didn't. She told me that I had an unusually bad case. In a state of scientific wonder, she decided to count the pox on my face one day, but she stopped just past the bridge of my nose, when she had already reached 100.*

*I was past the worst of it. The pox were scabbing over, and, though I was still sick, I felt so much better that I was filled with a kind of giddy exhilaration when I woke up that morning. I bound into the kitchen and told my mother that I was going to the basement to play with the puppies. She turned from the kitchen sink to face me and told me that one of the puppies had died during the night. "Why," I asked.*

*"You never know about these things," my mother replied. "So many things can be wrong that we can't even see."*

*"Where is the puppy?" I wanted to know.*

*"It's gone," she said.*

*"Gone where?" I wanted to know.*

*She didn't answer.*

*"Was it a boy or a girl?"*

*"It was a boy."*

*The next morning, I woke up a little earlier than usual. My mother stood in the kitchen, wrapping a tiny, still, black thing in a sheet of newspaper.*

*"You're up early," she said. "Another puppy died last night."*

*"I want to see it."*

*She unwrapped a corner of the newspaper, and I could see the fat, adorable-looking puppy that I had held and played with the day before. It was completely limp, like a rag doll. But otherwise—perfect. "How do you know it's dead?"*

*"Because I know," my mother said.*

*Eight. Seven. Six. Five. Four. Three. Two. One.*

*Every night, another puppy died. My mother said that Weimaraners were special dogs. A highly pure German breed. We had intended to breed Heidi with a carefully selected male, but she had gotten knocked up in the backyard before my parents knew that she was in heat. My mother explained that oftentimes, when Weimaraners bred with other types of dogs, the puppies were not viable. It was a new word—viable.*

*One puppy remained. A male. Each morning I woke up, and he was still alive. I studied him, trying to figure out what possible magic he possessed that allowed him to live. My parents found a young man who wanted to adopt him. My mother told me that he was going to come to our house in a couple of days and take the puppy to grow up and live with him.*

*"Are you sure he'll be able to stay alive," I asked. "Are you sure he's viable?"*

*"I'm sure," she said.*

*Now that I know the truth, I sometimes try to picture it. I wonder how my mother made her decision about which one she would choose. I picture her carrying a wriggling puppy in her hands, up the basement stairs and into our darkened kitchen. I see her plugging the drain and running a sink-full of water. Or did she run the water in advance? Warm, or cool? What goes through your mind when you are cradling new life in your hands, feeling that life drain away, watching for those last tiny bubbles of air to rise to the surface?*

## Chapter 43

***When*** the front door closed behind the moviegoers, a vast silence rang through the old house. The ghosts of the sounds of joyful carols, the plunks and twangs of John and Kate tuning up their instruments for holiday duets, even Madeline's humming while frosting the Christmas cakes—all of the sounds of the previous twenty-four hours shouted their departure. And the sad, angry sounds as well—the whispered phone conversations wafting from the far corners, the final clunk of Dan's fork on his breakfast plate as he threw it down, the sobs from behind Kate's door—these sounds withered and retreated into the shadows.

Madeline chose the silence, once again recognizing the company of ghosts.

The sounds of thirty Christmases reverberated through her head: John's and Kate's feet racing down the stairs on Christmas morning, each year's footfalls a bit louder than the last as they grew; the year Madeline struggled to fall asleep against a backdrop of distant beeps and pings from the video game

Santa Claus had set up for John; the year Kate was two and got a stuffed capuchin monkey that was half the size she was. A tag revealed its name to be Cappuccino; Kate misheard it as Cappu-puccino. She carried him everywhere, hugging him and saying his name over and over.

By the time Dylan awakened, the fire she had lit in the fireplace had burned down to a steady flame. She changed Dylan's diaper and swaddled him in a fresh blanket. "Well, look at us," she said. "It's Christmas Day, and I'm holding a brand-new baby, wrapped in swaddling clothes." Hungry though he was, he looked right into Madeline's eyes, and he smiled. His wobbly half smile, the curl of his tiny lip—these struck Madeline as the most beautiful things she had ever seen.

Something she had not thought of for many years came into her head. She saw her mother at the kitchen sink, holding a wriggling black puppy in her own two hands and waiting for its life to drain away. Its inconvenient, imperfect life.

John's words about Kate swirled into and around Madeline's head: *maybe she needs us to show her how.*

And Madeline thought about her own image of Claire—a girl standing on a little spit of land in the middle of the Niagara River, jaw set and arms akimbo, watching the torrent of churning water rushing past her and believing she could stem that flow.

*Maybe she needs us to show her how.*

"Beautiful boy," Madeline whispered to Dylan. "Beautiful, beautiful baby boy."

*It turns out I can't really push the river; I can't make it go in a different direction than it's going to go. I have no idea what crazy twists and turns your life may take. All I know is that you're here, and that matters. All I have to offer, all I've ever had to offer, is love. My messy, flawed, crazy-ass love.*

"I will do the best I can. I will."

# Epilogue

***Dylan*** is pounding on the window and jumping up and down as Madeline gets out of her car. She gives a hearty wave, first with one hand then with both, as Dylan continues to pound and jump and wave, all at once. Proust goes crazy when Madeline enters John and Claire's apartment, demanding immediate recognition and snorting in response to the minimal fussing Madeline gives him.

Dylan throws himself onto the couch, and sometimes onto the floor, dissolving in a fit of giggles, hopping through the apartment to gather the things he will pack in his giraffe backpack for their day together. He weighs which Thomas trains to stow away in his pack and which he will hold in his hand for the drive to Madeline's house. John buckles Dylan into his car seat with a wealth of kisses and gives Madeline an immense embrace. He always says, "Thanks, Ma," his name for her when he is at his most relaxed and happiest. And he adds, "Love you."

"Go over the bump-bumps!" Dylan says as soon as the two of them pull away from the curb. "Go fast over them!"

"Wheeeeeee!" Madeline says as they hit the first one. "Shall we do more speed bumps? Or, is that enough for today?"

"More speed bumps!"

All week Madeline looks forward to her Sundays with Dylan. Her friends tell her how lucky she is to have such an unusually close relationship with her foster grandson. Dan is long gone. He got on his airplane as planned, never seeing Madeline again after that fateful Christmas. He contacted her from Mexico, apologizing for having left town without so much as a word. He wanted to see her again he said. They had something rare and special and magical and magnificent he said. She said, more or less, "Fuck that noise." There were one or two after Dan, but no one who has struck the right chord, the chord that Madeline continues to hope—and sometimes to believe—is out there.

"I know," she says to her friends, "I know that I'm lucky."

*Here's what is known: Dylan was removed from Savannah's care when he was three months old. He spent the following month in a foster care center. Claire and John scrambled to become his temporary foster parents. As time went by, they applied to become full, legal guardians, and they have been raising Dylan—with an overflowing bounty of love, laughter, tears, worry, stress, strain, wackiness, exhaustion, and joy—ever since.*

*Here's what is unknown: everything.*

# *Acknowledgments*

Lest it become an overwhelming task to acknowledge my gratitude to the many people who played a meaningful role in bringing *Pushing the River* to its final form as a finished novel, I thought I'd go in chronological order. And, as I suppose there is strong tradition and precedent for thanking one's parents, I will join the ranks of beginning there. My parents led decent, but compromised, lives; and my perception of that engendered a persistence and determination that I am endlessly grateful to possess (except when it annoys me or drives me to do crazy shit).

I owe a great debt to the readers of the earliest drafts of the manuscript: Rita Dragonette, Clark Elliott, Jacki Marton, Karen Monier, Julie Oscherwitz-Grant, James R. Peterson, and Janis Post. Each one of you gave me strong encouragement and helpful feedback, despite having been handed a meandering, skeletal manuscript that possibly re-defined the very term "rough" draft.

Molly K. Hales was another of the early readers, and the one whose ideas and suggestions proved helpful beyond my wildest dreams. For anyone reading this who is a writer, here's a tip: find yourself a Ph.D. student in the humanities to read your manuscripts. Those people have been doing nothing but reading stuff about various aspects of the human condition, then dissecting, analyzing, discussing, and writing about those ideas for hours and hours every day for *years*. Find one! And with some luck, you will locate one who also has the depth and wisdom of Molly, and has been reading fiction voraciously enough that her elementary teachers complained about it. I cannot thank her enough for her ongoing help and support through every step of this.

My experience with my publishers, Amika Press, has been astonishing—wholly positive and totally seamless—and I know that this is rare, indeed. Jay Amberg, you founded the press that made a decision to take a chance on me. Bless you. Sarah Koz, your ideas about everything related to the design and production of the novel were spot on, and what's more, you were a pleasure to work with. John Manos, I am rather at a loss for words (haha). Your tireless work and devotion to my manuscript went so far beyond what I could have imagined. You took my breath away, time after time (rewrite after rewrite). Every time I got an email from you, I postponed reading it until I could carve out a time—knowing that my first response would be to cry. For a long time. Then, I would have to read your email, with its overarching suggestions, at least three more times over at least two more days trying to determine what the hell you were trying to say. When it finally gelled, when I finally "got it," I realized that you were, of course, right. Thank you, for your work and support and encouragement and insistence that I keep working, keep endeavoring to make *Pushing the River* the best book it could be.

Sarra Jahedi, you created a painting that was the perfect presentation for the cover of my book; and David Robbins, you found it.

Thanks to the folks on my book launch team, each of whom worked hard to get the word out about this novel: Laura Allen-Simpson, Meg Bauhof, Jan Seriff Berger, Ruth Hull Chatlien, Deborah Good, Marty Hales, Bill Horstman, Steven A. Jones, Glenda Kapsalis, Debbie Pavick, James A. Peterson, Melissa Ann Pinney, David A. Robbins, Mary Weismantel and Gary Wilson (plus Karen Monier, Julie Oscherwitz-Grant and Janis Post).

Finally, I want to thank Taylor, Michelle and Dawson, mostly for, well, for being Taylor, Michelle and Dawson. You are the reason.

## *About the Author*

***Barbara Monier*** has been writing since her earliest days when she composed in crayon on paper with extremely wide lines. She studied writing at Yale University and the University of Michigan. While at Michigan, she received the Avery and Jule Hopwood Prize. It was the highest prize awarded that year and the first in Michigan's history for a piece written directly for the screen. *Pushing the River* is the latest of her three novels. *You, In Your Green Shirt* and *A Little Birdie Told Me* (available on Amazon) are her previous titles.

## *About the Artist*

Self Taug't, I Pain'td

A'Impartial'd Language.

A'Warn Of Talent.

I' Un†imeth.

SarraJahedi.com

Made in the USA
Lexington, KY
14 September 2019